'I'm pretty sure it's against the law to break a contract with the nation's ruler.' Her laugh was hollow. 'Besides...' she lifted her head and looked him straight in the eye '...what man would dare steal the Emir's bride? He'd be punished, surely?'

Soraya's upturned face was beautiful, her eyes almost beseeching, and Zahir knew a crazy urge to kiss her till the world faded and all that was left was them.

'He'd lose all claim to honour or loyalty to the crown.' Zahir said slowly, feeling the full weight of such a prospect. He'd made honour and loyalty his life. 'He'd never be able to hold his head up again. He'd be stripped of official titles and positions and the council of elders would banish him from Bakhara.' He drew a deep breath. 'Hussein could never call him friend again.'

'As I thought.' Her hands dropped and she stepped abruptly out of his hold. 'No man would even consider it.'

Annie West spent her childhood with her nose between the covers of a book—a habit she retains. After years preparing government reports and official correspondence she decided to write something she *really* enjoys. And there's nothing she loves more than a great romance. Despite her office-bound past she has managed a few interesting moments—including a marriage offer with the promise of a herd of camels to sweeten the contract. She is happily married to her ever-patient husband (who has never owned a dromedary). They live with their two children amongst the tall eucalypts at beautiful Lake Macquarie, on Australia's east coast. You can e-mail Annie at www.annie-west.com, or write to her at PO Box 1041, Warners Bay, NSW 2282, Australia.

Recent titles by the same author:

UNDONE BY HIS TOUCH
GIRL IN THE BEDOUIN TENT
PRINCE OF SCANDAL
PASSION, PURITY AND THE PRINCE

Did you know these are also available as eBooks?
Visit www.millsandboon.co.uk

DEFYING HER DESERT DUTY

BY
ANNIE WEST

MILLS &
BOON

First published in Great Britain 2012
by Mills & Boon, an imprint of Harlequin (UK) Limited.
Harlequin (UK) Limited, Eton House, 18-24 Paradise Road,
Richmond, Surrey TW9 1SR

© Annie West 2012

ISBN: 978 0 263 22808 3

DEFYING HER DESERT DUTY

CHAPTER ONE

He was watching her.

Still.

Soraya's nape prickled. A ripple of hot sensation skated down her arms. She fought the need to look up, knowing what she'd see.

The man in the shadows.

Big. Dark. Broad-shouldered in his leather jacket, the hard lines of his face a study in masculine strength. His upper face was in shadow yet every time she looked across the dimly lit bar there was no doubt his gaze was fixed on her. She felt the intensity of that look in her sizzling blood. And in the curious breathless catch in her throat.

His interest unsettled Soraya. She leaned closer to her group: Raoul and Jean Paul debating politics while Michelle and Marie talked fashion. Raoul roped a negligent arm around her shoulders. Instantly she stiffened, then forced herself to relax, reminding herself it was just a friendly gesture.

Soraya loved Paris's casual lifestyle, but still hadn't overcome her reserve. You could take the girl out of Bakhara but Bakhara still lingered in the girl. Her lips twisted. She'd no need of the chaperone her father had wanted to send.

Movement caught her eye and despite her intentions she turned.

He hadn't moved; he still leaned back just beyond the flickering light of the candle on his table. But now he looked up at a leggy blonde in a red satin mini-dress. The woman leaned in, her low-cut neckline a blatant invitation.

Soraya snapped her head back to her friends, ignoring the way Raoul tightened his hold.

Zahir sank back in his chair and cradled his drink, its cool condensation a respite from the heat. A heat that owed nothing to the close atmosphere of the nightclub and everything to the woman on the other side of the room.

What the devil had he walked into?

Simple, Hussein had said. Straightforward.

Zahir shook his head. Every sense screamed 'alert'. Every instinct warned of trouble.

Still he remained. He had no choice. Now he'd found her, he couldn't leave.

He tipped his head back so the ice slid into his mouth. He crunched it hard, as if the shock of cold might restore his equanimity.

It would take more than ice to counteract his tension.

In other circumstances he might have taken up the invitation of the voluptuous Swedish girl in the short dress. He enjoyed life's pleasures—in his down time.

Never at the expense of his duty.

Tonight was duty, responsibility, obligation.

Yet it was something more too. Something…unfamiliar, evoked by sloe-dark eyes and a full Cupid's bow mouth. By the woman hanging on the words of a scrawny intellectual pontificating as if he had any idea how to run a country!

Zahir snorted and put down his glass.

Whatever it was he felt, he didn't like it. It was a complication he didn't need. Zahir had spent a lifetime learning how to cut through complications.

Over the years he'd learned to curb his impatience. Now he mostly used a statesman's skills: negotiation and discretion. But he'd trained as a warrior from birth. He was still technically head of the Emir's bodyguard, a position that gave opportunities for the satisfaction of hard, physical combat. The clash of one man against another.

He surveyed the *poseur* who was boasting of his intellect and pulling the woman in the dark dress close. The Frenchman's hand hovered near her bare arm. Zahir's fist tightened.

He'd like to get his hands on that buffoon and give him a short, sharp lesson in the real meaning of power.

The intensity of his bloodlust brought him up short.

Premonition skittered like icy fingers down his spine.

This mission was a mistake. He felt it in his bones.

Soraya moved back as far as Raoul's encircling arms allowed.

It was ridiculously late and she'd rather be home in bed. Except her flatmate Lisle had finally made peace with her boyfriend and Soraya knew they needed privacy, even if it meant staying out till dawn. Lisle had been a good friend and friendship was something precious to her.

But she'd made a mistake, finally agreeing to dance with Raoul. She frowned and shifted his straying hand.

Usually Soraya didn't make such mistakes. Keeping her distance from men came naturally. She'd acted out of character, spooked by the need to escape the stranger's unnerving stare. It had made her feel...heated. Aware.

Yet even now she felt his gaze like a brand on her back, her bare arms, her cheeks.

What did he *want*? She wasn't eye-catching. Her dress was modest—positively maidenly, Lisle would say.

Soraya wanted to march across the room and demand he stop it. But this was Paris. Men stared at women all the time. It was a national pastime.

Raoul's marauding hand cut her line of thought and she stiffened. Enough was enough. 'Stop it! Move your hand or—'

'The lady is ready for a change, I believe.' The voice, a deep burr, curled around her like a caress, but there was no mistaking its steely undertone.

Raoul stumbled to a halt then stepped back abruptly as a

large hand removed his arm from Soraya's waist. His eyes flared as he drew himself up. Yet, tall as he was, the stranger topped him easily.

Raoul spluttered as he was shouldered aside. Soraya felt the tensile strength in the intruder's big body as he clasped her in a waltz hold and swung her away.

Torn between relief at being rid of Raoul's octopus hands and stomach-dipping shock at the newcomer's actions, protest froze in Soraya's throat.

It was *him*, the man who'd watched her all evening.

Suddenly he was so near, his breath feathered her forehead, the heat of his body warmed hers and his big hands grasped her so easily it was obvious he was used to being close to a woman.

Soraya shivered as an unfamiliar sensation swirled deep. Not trepidation. Not indignation. But something that tied her thoughts in knots and prompted her to fall in step unthinkingly as he moved to the slow tune.

'Now just you wait—' Over the stranger's shoulder she saw Raoul's face, red with indignation, his fist raised. Soraya's eyes widened. Could he be violent?

'Raoul! No! That's enough.'

'Excuse me a moment.' The stranger released her, swung round to confront Raoul and said something under his breath that made the graduate student pale and falter back a pace.

Then, before she had time to question, he turned back, gathered her to him and swung her across the dance floor.

It was an impressive example of a male staking his territory. But Soraya didn't appreciate being swept away without so much as a by-your-leave.

Even if he had rescued her from Raoul's pawing.

'There's no need for this.' She'd rather just get off the dance floor. But he gave no indication he'd heard.

It chagrined her that her feet automatically followed his lead. She'd never followed *any* man, except her beloved father!

She could wrench herself from his arms and off the dance

floor, but she shied from making more of a scene unless absolutely necessary.

Besides, she was curious.

'What makes you think I want to dance with you?' She jutted her chin defiantly to counteract the strange, breathy quality of her voice.

The movement was a mistake. With her face tilted, her gaze collided with sizzling dark-emerald fire. Shock jolted her and only quick reflexes kept her from stumbling.

His eyes were heavy-lidded, almost lazy. Yet there was nothing lazy about his rapier-sharp scrutiny. She sucked in a breath as it roved her face.

His features were compelling. Strong, with an earthy stamp of male sexuality that melded with sharp cheekbones, a determined jaw and a long blade of a nose to create a breathtaking whole. His skin was dark gold, eyes rayed with the tiny lines that spoke of hours spent outdoors. She couldn't believe they were smile lines. Not on this man who surveyed her so grimly.

Soraya blinked and tore her gaze away, disturbed to find her pulse skittering faster.

'You weren't *enjoying* your dance with him?' He shrugged and she knew in that moment that, despite his perfect French, he wasn't local. There was none of the Gallic insouciance in that movement. Instead she read the fluid yet deliberate action of a man who had more on his mind than a little light flirtation.

He moved with a lithe grace yet every action, from the way he held her hand to the light clasp of his other palm at her waist, was carefully controlled.

For all his agility he was a big man, all hard-packed muscle, iron-hard sinew and bone. Formidable.

Suddenly she felt…trapped, at risk. Ridiculous, since she was in full public view with her friends close by.

Desperately she sucked in a deep breath and sought out her companions. They watched, rapt, elbows on the table and mouths moving as if they'd never seen anything more fascinating than Soraya dancing, and with a stranger. As her eyes met Raoul's, he flushed and moved closer to Marie.

'That's not the point.'

'So you don't disagree. He was annoying you.' His voice was low yet she had an inkling he worked to keep his tone easy.

'I don't need a protector!' Soraya prided herself on her independence.

'Then why didn't you stop him grabbing at you?' There was no mistaking the thread of anger in that deep voice, or the quiver of repressed power that rippled through him in a rolling tide.

It was her turn to shrug.

What was there to say? That despite the freedom of studying abroad she wasn't used to dealing with groping hands? She usually kept a discreet distance from male colleagues. Soraya had perfected the art of blending into a crowd and avoiding individual male attention. Tonight was the first time she'd ever danced with a man.

No way was she confessing that! It was the norm for a well-brought-up girl in Bakhara. Here it would make her seem like a freak.

As would the fact she preferred it that way. She had no interest in a love affair.

'Nothing to say?'

'What I do is none of your business.'

At her words his lips firmed, deep lines bracketing a mobile mouth that revealed tension despite his air of command. One sleek black eyebrow climbed towards close-cropped dark hair.

That superior look would goad any woman's patience.

The music finished and they slowed to a stop.

'Thank you for the dance.' Formal politeness barely masked her annoyance. How dared he suggest she should be thankful to him?

She turned and took a step away, only to find his hold tightening at her waist. Long fingers and a broad palm seared through the soft fabric of her dress, warming her in a way that suddenly seemed too intimate.

The music resumed and with a swift movement he tugged her close so she stumbled against a hard wall of hot muscle.

'What the—?'

'What if I choose to make it my business?' His breath was warm on her face. Those straight eyebrows arrowed down in a scowl that accentuated the intensity of his blazing green stare.

It was as if he memorised everything, from her too-short nose and plain brown eyes to the wisps of hair escaping her once-neat chignon.

The intensity of that look dazed her. 'Sorry?'

'You heard me, princess. Don't play games.'

'Play games?' She shook her head, her jaw clenching in indignation. She planted her hands against his upper arms, trying to prise herself free, and felt only unyielding steel. 'I've done nothing! It's you playing games. Sitting there all night, just watching me.'

Her eyes met his again and her chest tightened at the simmering heat she saw there. Her skin tingled all over.

'You wanted me to do more than watch?' His words were a whispered thread of frayed velvet. 'Is that why you cosied up to your friend over there—to trigger a response?'

'No!' Soraya rocked back on her heels, but his arm at her waist, like a rope of steel, lashed her to him.

For an instant she read something in his gaze, something half-hidden that both disturbed and fascinated.

Then she came to her senses. With a swift, well-executed movement she ground her stiletto heel onto his instep with all her weight.

A moment later she was free. His hand fell away and with it the warmth at her waist she'd almost grown used to.

She strode from the dance floor, head up and shoulders back. A woman in control.

But at the back of her mind lingered the image of his face when she'd fought to break free. There'd been no flicker of pain in his eyes, no hint of a wince on his face, despite what must have been piercing agony.

What sort of man trained himself not to react to pain?

The question unnerved her.

So did the realisation she was only free because he'd *chosen* to release her.

Holding her in his arms had been a mistake.

Zahir grimaced and ruthlessly shoved aside any analysis of *why* it was a mistake.

No need to go there. All that mattered was that she was trouble with a capital T.

He'd known it when he'd arrived at her apartment and found, not the respectable accommodation he'd expected, but a love nest for an almost-naked couple. Clearly they'd tumbled out of bed only because his insistent ringing of the bell had threatened to attract the neighbours.

His assessment had been reinforced when he'd finally tracked her to this seedy club. True, she didn't flaunt herself half-naked like some women. But that dress, the colour of ripe plums, clung lovingly to curves designed to snare a man's attention. Its skirt flirted and flounced around shapely legs when she moved. It slithered enticingly under a man's palm, making him itch to explore further.

Zahir swallowed a curse as his palms tingled.

This wasn't about what she made him feel.

He wasn't in the business of feeling *anything* for her.

Except disgust that she'd played Hussein for a fool. Look at the way she'd snuggled up to that turkey with the ridiculously sculpted excuse for a beard!

He stifled a low growl of anger.

No, she was *not* what he'd been led to believe. And he didn't just mean the fact that the old photo he'd been given showed the round, almost chubby face of an innocent. The woman tonight had the cheekbones, sexy curves and full, pouting lips of a born seductress. And those shoes—spangled four-inch stilettos that screamed *'take me...now!'*.

Heat pooled low. Disgust, he assured himself.

The one time she'd impressed was when she'd stood up to him. Few people dared do that.

The look in her eye when she'd used that damned spike heel had, for a moment, arrested him. And the way she'd strode back across the dance floor, with the grace and hauteur of an empress, had made him want to applaud.

At least she had guts. She was no push-over.

The determined click of feminine heels snared his attention and he straightened from the wall.

Instantly the rhythm of those footsteps slowed and a disturbing fire sparked in his blood. He'd felt it each time her eyes collided with his.

Hell! Now he felt it from her mere glance.

A volatile mixture of fury, guilt and some other darker emotion surged to the surface.

This was *not* the way it should be. Zahir refused to countenance it.

He swung round to face her across the foyer of the nightclub. At this hour even the bouncer had deserted his post. They were alone.

'You! What are you doing here?' Her hand crept to her throat, then, as if recognising that for a sign of weakness, she dropped it to her side and lifted her chin. Subtly she widened her stance. What, did she mean to kick him in the groin if he tried to approach her?

It would do her no good, of course. Overpowering her would be a moment's work.

But that wasn't an option. Despite her flaws, she would be treated with respect. That was why he'd waited till they had privacy to approach her.

He ignored that ill-advised, inexplicable impulse to approach her on the dance floor.

'We need to talk.'

But already she was shaking her head. Flyaway strands of dark chocolate tresses swirled around her slender throat.

Zahir forced his focus to her eyes. Dark as ebony, they held his unflinchingly. He gave her full marks for bravado.

'We have nothing to discuss.' Her gaze skated across his shoulders, his chest and back up again. 'If you don't leave me alone I'll—'

'What? Call out for lover-boy to rescue you?' He crossed his arms over his chest and saw her gaze follow the movement. The low simmer of heat in his veins became a sizzle, igniting a temper he'd almost forgotten he had.

What was it about this woman that got under his skin? It was unheard of.

'No.' She took a mobile phone from her purse and flipped it open. 'I'll call the police.'

'Not a wise move, princess.'

'*Don't* call me that!' She quivered with outrage, her mouth a pout of wrathful indignation.

Too late, Zahir realised why he'd baited her.

Not because she deserved it.

Not because he was naturally crass.

But because he wanted her to look at him, respond to him, as she had on the dance floor. There, despite her defiant words, her body had melted against his just for a moment in an unspoken invitation as old as time.

Hell and damnation!

What was he playing at?

'Forgive me, Ms Karim.' Carefully he blanked his expression, speaking in the modulated tones he used when brokering a particularly difficult negotiation.

'You know my name!' She stumbled back a half-step, alarm in her eyes.

Registering her fear, Zahir tasted self-disgust on his tongue. Nothing he'd done tonight had gone as intended. Where was his professionalism, his years of experience handling the most difficult and delicate missions?

'You have nothing to fear.' He spread his palms in an open gesture.

But she backed up another step, groping behind her for the door into the bar. 'I don't hold conversations with strange men in places like this.' Her gesture encompassed the empty foyer.

Zahir drew a deep breath. 'Not even a man who comes direct from your bridegroom?'

CHAPTER TWO

SORAYA froze, muscles cramping in shock as that one word reverberated through her stunned brain.

Bridegroom...

No, no! Not yet. Not now. She wasn't ready.

Her heart rose in her throat, clogging her airways, lurching out of kilter. Her senses swam. It couldn't be. She had months yet here in Paris—hadn't she?

Soraya staggered back till the hand behind her met a solid surface. Fingers splayed, she pressed into the wall, needing its support.

Through hazy vision she registered abrupt movement: the stranger striding across the small space, arm raised as if to reach for her.

She stiffened and he slammed to a halt, his hand dropping. This close she should be able to read his expression but in the dim light his features looked like they'd been carved from harsh stone, betraying nothing. His eyes blazed, but with what she couldn't discern.

At least he didn't touch her again.

She didn't want his hand on her. She didn't like the curious heat that stirred when he did.

She dragged in a deep breath, then another, trying to calm her racing pulse. With him so close, watching like an eagle sighting its prey, it was impossible. She had nowhere to retreat to. And even if she did she knew he'd follow.

He had the grim, resolute aura of a man who finished what he started.

Her heart give a little jagged thump and she forced herself to stand tall. Even in her new shoes she still had to tilt her head to meet his gaze. He was big—broad across the shoulder and tall. Yet his physical size was only part of the impact. There was something in his eyes...

Soraya jerked her gaze away.

'You've come from Bakhara?' Her voice was husky.

'I have.'

She opened her mouth to ask if he'd come direct from *him*, but the words disintegrated in her dry mouth. It was stupid, but for as long as she didn't say the words she could almost pretend it wasn't true.

Yet even in denial Soraya couldn't pretend this was a mistake. The man before her wasn't the sort to make mistakes. That poised, lethal stillness spoke a language all its own. There'd be no errors with this man. She shivered, cold to the bones.

'And you are?' Soraya forced herself to speak.

One slashing black eyebrow rose, as if he recognised her question for the delay tactic it was.

'My name is Zahir Adnan El Hashem.' He sketched an elegant bow that confirmed his story more definitively than any words. It proclaimed him totally at home with the formal etiquette of the royal court.

In jeans, boots and black leather, the movement should have looked out of place, but somehow the casual western clothes only reinforced his hard strength and unyielding posture. And made her think of formidable desert fighters.

Soraya swallowed hard, her flesh chilling.

She'd heard of Zahir El Hashem. Who in Bakhara hadn't? He was the Emir's right-hand man. A force to be reckoned with: a renowned warrior and, according to her father, a man fast developing a reputation in the region as a canny but well-regarded diplomat.

Her fingers threaded into a taut knot.

She'd thought he'd be older, given his reputation. But what made her tense was the fact that the Emir had sent *him*, his most trusted royal advisor. A man rumoured to be as close to the Emir as family. A man known not for kindness but for his uncompromising strength. A man who'd have no compunction about hauling home an unwilling bride.

Her heart sank.

It was true, then. Absolutely, irrefutably true.

Her future had caught up with her.

The future she'd hoped might never eventuate.

'And you are Soraya Karim.'

It wasn't a question. He knew exactly who she was.

And hated her for it, she realised with a flash of disturbing insight as something flickered in the sea-green depths of those remarkable eyes.

No, not hatred. Something else.

Finally she found her voice, no matter that it was raspy with shock. 'Why seek me out here? It's hardly a suitable time to meet.'

His other eyebrow rose and heat flooded her cheeks. He knew she was prevaricating. Did he realise she'd do almost anything not to hear the news he brought?

'What I have to say is important.'

'I have no doubt.' She dragged her hand from the supporting wall and made a show of flicking shut her phone and putting it away. 'But surely we could discuss it tomorrow at a civilised time?' She was putting off the inevitable and probably sounding like a spoiled brat in the bargain. But she couldn't help it. Her blood chilled at the thought of what he'd come all this way to tell her.

'It's already tomorrow.'

And he wasn't going anywhere. His stance said it all.

'You have no interest in my message?' He paused, his eyes boring into her as if looking for something he couldn't find. 'You're not concerned with the possibility that I bring bad news?' His face remained unreadable but there was no mistaking the sharp edge to his voice.

The phone clattered to the floor from Soraya's nerveless fingers.

'My father?' Her hand shot to her mouth, pressing against trembling lips.

'No!' Colour deepened the razor-sharp line of his cheekbones. He shook his head emphatically. 'No. Your father is well. I'm sorry. I shouldn't have—'

'If not my father, then—?'

An abrupt gesture stopped her words. 'My apologies, Ms Karim. I should not have mentioned the possibility. It was thoughtless of me. Let me assure you, everyone close to you is well.'

Close to her. That included the man who'd sent him.

Suddenly, looking into the stormy depths of Zahir El Hashem's eyes, Soraya realised why he'd pushed her. How unnatural of any woman not to be concerned that sudden news might bring bad tidings about the man she was supposed to spend the rest of her life with.

Guilt hit her. How unnatural *was* she? Surely she cared about him? He deserved no less. Yet these last months she'd almost fooled herself into believing that future might never come to pass.

No wonder his emissary looked at her so searchingly. Had her response, or lack of it, given her away?

'I'm glad to hear it,' she murmured, ducking her head to cover the confusion she felt. At her feet lay her phone. She bent to retrieve it only to find her hand meeting his as he scooped the phone up.

His hand was hard, callused, broad of palm and long-fingered. The hand of a man who, despite his familiarity with the royal court, did far more with his days than consider protocol.

The touch of his flesh, warm and so different from her own, made her retreat instinctively, her breath sucking in on a gasp.

Or was it the memory of that same hand holding her tight against him on the dance floor? Fire snaked through her veins, making her aware of him as *male*.

'Your phone.'

'Thank you.' She kept her eyes averted, not wanting to face his searching stare again.

'Again, I apologise for my clumsiness. For letting you fear—'

'It's all right. No harm done.' Soraya shook her head, wishing it was the case, when all she could think of was that her reaction betrayed her as thoughtless, ungrateful, not deserving the good fortune she'd so enjoyed.

Worse, it was proof positive the doubts she'd begun to harbour had matured into far more than vague dissatisfaction and pie-in-the-sky wishing.

'Come,' he said, his voice brusque. 'We can't discuss this here.'

Reluctantly Soraya raised her head, taking in the deserted foyer, the muffled music from the club and the mingled scents of cigarette smoke, perfume and sweat.

He was right. She needed to hear the details.

She nodded, exhaustion engulfing her. It was the exhaustion a cornered animal must feel, facing its predator at the end of a long hunt from which there was no escape.

She felt spent. Vulnerable.

Soraya straightened her shoulders. 'Of course.'

He ushered her out and she felt the warmth of his hand at her back, close but not touching. Something in the quiver of tension between them told her he wouldn't touch her again. She was grateful for it.

Fingers of pale grey spread across the dawn sky, vying with the streetlights in the deserted alley. She looked around for a long, dark, official-looking vehicle. The place was deserted but for a big motorbike in the shadows.

Where to? She couldn't take him home; not with Lisle

and her boyfriend there. The place was roomy but the walls were thin.

'This way.' He ushered her towards the main road then down another side street with a sureness that told her he knew exactly where he was going.

She supposed she should have asked for proof of identity before following him. But she dismissed the thought as another delaying tactic. There was no doubt in her mind that he was who he said.

Besides, she felt like she'd gone three rounds in a boxing ring already. And this had only just started! How would she cope?

A shudder rippled down her spine.

A moment later weighted warmth encompassed her. She faltered to a stop. Around her shoulders swung a man's heavy leather jacket, lined with soft fabric that held the heat of his body and the clean fragrance of male skin.

Soraya's nostrils flared as her senses dipped and whirled, dizzy with the invasion of her space and the onslaught of unfamiliar reactions.

'You were cold.' His words were clipped. In the gloom his face was unreadable, but his stance proclaimed his distance, mental as well as physical.

He stood tall, the dark fabric of his T-shirt skimming a torso taut with leashed energy. His hands curled and the muscles in his arms bunched, revealing the blatant power his jacket had concealed. Resolutely she stopped her eyes skimming lower to those long denim-clad legs.

He looked potent. *Dangerous.*

'Thank you.' Soraya forced her gaze away, down the street that had begun to stir with carriers hefting boxes. A street market was beginning to take shape.

Relief welled. Surrounded by other people, surely the unfamiliar sensations she felt alone with him would dissipate? She'd been like a cat on burning sand for hours, all because of him.

She dragged his jacket in around her shoulders, telling herself the shock of news from Bakhara unnerved her. Her sense of unreality had nothing to do with the man so stonily silent beside her.

Zahir shortened his pace to match hers. She had long legs but those heels weren't made for cobblestones. They slowed her walk to a provocative hip-tilting sway far slower than his usual stride.

Resolutely he kept his eyes fixed ahead, not on her undulating walk.

Heat seared his throat and tightened his belly. How could he have been so stupid? So thoughtless? The look on her face when she'd thought he brought bad news about her father had punched a fist of guilt right through his belly.

Damn him for a blundering fool!

All because he'd judged her and found her wanting. Because she wasn't eager to hear the news from Hussein. Because she didn't care what tidings he brought if they interfered with her night out.

Because she wasn't the woman he'd presumed her to be, a woman worthy of Hussein.

Not when she spent the night snuggling up to another man, dancing with him, bewitching him with those enormous, lustrous eyes. Letting him paw her as if he owned her.

Zahir cupped the back of his neck, massaging it to ease the tension there.

Resolutely he shoved aside the whisper of suspicion that he'd have welcomed the chance to keep her in his own arms, feel her lush body pressed close.

This wasn't about him.

It was about her.

And the man to whom he owed everything.

'Thank you.' Soraya hugged the jacket close as he stood aside, holding open the door to a brightly lit café.

Entering, she felt she'd strayed back in time a century.

Wooden booths lined the walls, topped with mirrors etched in lush *art nouveau* designs. There were brass fittings of an earlier age, burnished and welcoming, and posters from a time when women wore corsets and men sported boaters or top hats.

But the whoosh of the gleaming coffee machine was modern, as was the sultry smile the petite, female *barista* bestowed on Zahir.

Something tweaked tight in Soraya's stomach. A thread of annoyance.

No wonder he was so sure of himself. He must take feminine adulation as his due.

Not this female.

Her heels clacked across the black-and-white tiled floor, giving the pretence of a confidence she didn't feel. Her legs shook and each step was an effort.

Sliding into a cushioned seat she focused on the café rather than the man who sat down opposite her.

If she'd had to guess she'd have said he'd favour a place that was sleek, dark and anonymous. Somewhere edgy, like him. Not a café that was traditional and comforting with its beautiful fittings and aura of quiet bustle.

A waitress had followed them to their table, her eyes on Zahir as they ordered.

He was worth looking at, Soraya grudgingly admitted, averting her gaze from his hard, sculpted jaw with its intriguing hint of morning shadow.

'You've come all the way from Bakhara,' she said flatly when they were alone. 'Why?'

She needed to hear it spelled out, even though there was only one reason he could be here.

'I come with a message from the Emir.'

Soraya nodded, swallowing a lump in her dry throat. Tension drilled down her spine. 'And?'

'The Emir sends greetings and enquires after your well-being.'

She speared him with a look. An enquiry after her health?

That could have been done through her father, who updated the Emir on her progress. Suddenly she was impatient to hear the worst. The delay notched her tension higher.

'I'm well.' She kept her tone even, despite the fact she couldn't seem to catch her breath. 'And the Emir? I hope he is in good health.'

'The Emir is in excellent health.' It was the expected response in the polite give-and-take of formal courtesy.

The sort of courtesy that had been so completely lacking in her dealings with this man.

Soraya's heart pulsed quicker as she recalled those overpowering emotions—the fury and indignation, the compulsion to know more, the feel of his gaze on her. The blast of untrammelled awareness when he'd held her.

She blinked and looked away.

Silence thickened, broken only by the eager waitress returning with their coffees: espresso for him, *café crème* for her. Automatically her hands wrapped round the oversized cup and she tilted her head, inhaling the steamy scent of hot cream and fragrant coffee.

'The Emir also sent me with news.'

Soraya nodded and lifted the cup to her lips, needing its heat. Even draped in his jacket she was cold. Cold with a chill that had nothing to do with the room temperature and everything to do with the creeping frost that crackled through her senses. The chill of foreboding.

'He asks that you accompany me to Bakhara. It's time for your wedding.'

Her slim fingers cupped the bowl of milky coffee so tightly Zahir saw them whiten. She didn't look up, but kept her eyes fixed on her drink. Following her gaze, he saw the creamy liquid ripple dangerously as her hands shook.

Instinct bade him reach out before she spilled the hot coffee and burned her hands.

Sense made him keep his hands to himself.

Bad enough that he knew the feel of her in his arms. Worse that he'd wanted…

No! He thrust the insidious thought aside.

Tiredness was to blame. The freedom of travelling the open road on his bike was what he'd needed after weeks locked in diplomatic negotiation on Hussein's behalf. But it had been a long journey.

As for the hum of awareness deep in his belly—it was a while since he'd shared his bed. That was all.

'I see.' Still she didn't look up. Nor did she drink. Instead she slowly lowered the coffee to the table, her hands still clamped round it as if for warmth.

Zahir frowned.

'Are you all right?' The words were tugged from his lips before he realised it.

Her mouth quirked up in a lopsided smile that somehow lacked humour. 'Perfectly, thank you.'

She lifted her head slowly, as if it was an effort.

Yet when her eyes met his he read nothing in them but a slight shimmer, as if the coffee's steam had made her eyes water. They were remarkable eyes. In the gloom of the club he'd thought them ebony. Here in the light he realised they were a dark, velvety brown, rich with a smattering of lighter specks, like gold dust.

Zahir sat back abruptly and lifted his espresso. Pungent and rich, the liquid seared his mouth and cleared his head.

'The Emir has set a date for the wedding?' Her voice was cool and crisp, yet he sensed strain there. Just as he saw strain in the rigid set of her neck and shoulders.

He shrugged. 'No date was mentioned to me.' As if Hussein would consult him on the minor details of his nuptials! That was what wedding planners were for. No doubt there were hordes of them, eager to have a hand in what would be the wedding of the decade.

'But…' She frowned and caught her bottom lip between her teeth. Resolutely he shifted his gaze from her lush mouth and turned to survey the café. It was doing a roaring trade in early-morning coffees for the market workers eager for a take-away caffeine fix. Yet here at the rear Zahir and his companion were totally alone.

'The Emir wants me to return?'

Hadn't he just said so? Zahir turned and found himself drowning in dark eyes that, if he didn't know better, he'd say held fear.

Nonsense. What was there to fear? Any woman would be ecstatic with the news he'd come to take her back to marry the Emir of Bakhara. If Hussein's character weren't enough to attract any woman, his personal wealth, not to mention his position of supreme authority, were bonuses few women could resist.

Soraya Karim had nothing to fear and everything to gain.

'He does.'

Zahir watched her shift in her seat. Her shoulders straightened, banishing the hint of a slump. Her chin lifted and her posture morphed into one of cool composure. Like the woman who'd stalked away from him in the club.

His heart gave a kick of appreciation and the dormant fire in his veins smouldered anew.

Hell! Since when had any woman had such an effect on him? Not even his last lover, naked and eager in his bed, would have garnered such an instantaneous response.

He rubbed his hand across his jaw, noting the stubble he hadn't bothered to remove. Lack of sleep was the problem. He'd been awake for thirty-six hours—eager to get here and get this over quickly so he could return to the new challenge that awaited him.

His reactions were haywire.

'The Emir has asked me to escort you home.' He curved his mouth in a reassuring smile and reined in his impatience—as if he had nothing better to do with his time than act as her minder on the trip from Paris to Bakhara.

Yet he couldn't begrudge Hussein this favour. Soraya Karim

would soon be his bride—of course he wanted her kept safe on the journey.

A pity no-one had thought to keep an eye on her while she partied in Paris!

'I thank the Emir for his kindness in providing an escort.' Her smile didn't reach her eyes. 'However, it would have been helpful if you'd contacted me before you arrived. That would have given me time to prepare.'

Zahir frowned at the hint of disapproval in her carefully polite tone.

What was there to prepare? Surely, as an eager bride, she'd jump at the chance to return to Bakhara and the opulent bridal gifts Hussein would shower upon her.

After years of delay Hussein was finally ready to proceed with the wedding. His chosen bride should be grinning with delight.

Instead she surveyed Zahir coolly.

'I'm here to assist. You can leave the details to me.' Winding up the lease on her apartment and organising a team of removalists would be the work of a few phone calls.

She nodded. 'I'm obliged to you. However, I prefer to make my own arrangements.' She paused. 'When is the Emir expecting me?'

'I've organised a flight tomorrow night. The royal jet will fly us back.' A day to complete his nursemaid duties and deliver her safely to Hussein. Then Zahir could make his way to his new post. He'd been itching to get to it for weeks.

'The Emir expects me *tomorrow*?' Her face leached of colour, leaving her looking unexpectedly fragile.

Zahir opened his mouth then shut it again.

This wasn't going to plan. He'd envisaged her eager to return to Bakhara and embrace her new life as wife of the country's ruler. He'd expected excitement, gratitude, even.

Instead she looked horrified.

A thread of curiosity curled within him till he blanked it out. He wasn't interested in understanding Soraya Karim, especially as he had a fair idea he wouldn't like what he found on closer inspection. He prized loyalty above all things and Hussein deserved better than a fiancée who couldn't be trusted to keep away from other men.

'There's a problem with tomorrow?' He didn't bother to hide his disapproval.

His nostrils flared with distaste as he wondered if she needed extra time to say goodbye to that lanky fool from the nightclub. Surely she wouldn't delay her departure for *him*? Or had he been a ploy? Perhaps she'd been trying to make the handsome blond guy at their table jealous.

He'd observed the covetous glances she'd attracted in that bar. Anger stirred at the notion she'd played fast and loose with Hussein's trust.

'No, tomorrow's not convenient.' Just that. No explanations, no apologies, just a shimmer of defiance in those fine eyes and a hint of mulish wilfulness in her down-turned mouth.

Despite himself, Zahir felt a spark of appreciation for the way she stonewalled him. The negotiators this last week could have done with some of her spunk. They might have come out of the joint-venture deal with a better share of the profits.

But that didn't negate the fact that she disrupted his plans. True, Hussein hadn't specified a date for his bride's return, but Zahir wanted to conclude this task and move on to his new role. He hadn't been so eager for anything in years.

'And when will it be *convenient*?'

Colour rose in her cheeks and her lips parted as if to protest his curt tone. Zahir's pulse missed a beat and heat combusted deep in his belly as he watched her mouth turn from sulky to an enticing O. With his jacket pulled around her shoulders and her hair coming down in soft curling tresses, she looked inviting, available, *tempting*.

Not like the fiancée of his mentor and best friend.

Her eyes widened as if she read his response despite the savage control he exerted to keep it hidden.

The tension between them notched higher. It trembled in the

air, a pressure that had more do with his reaction to her than with the subject under discussion.

This couldn't be!

It *wouldn't* be.

By hook or by crook he'd have her back in Bakhara, safe with her fiancé and out of his life, before her feet could touch the ground.

CHAPTER THREE

SORAYA knew disapproval when she saw it.

Despite his almost expressionless face, that flat, accusing stare said everything his words didn't.

If it hadn't been imprinted on her so early perhaps she'd never have recognised it. But nothing, not time or distance, could erase the memory of her father's relatives whispering and tutting over the sordid details of her mother's misdemeanours— or their certainty that, if unchecked, Soraya would go the same way to ruin. Even the servants gossiped in delighted condemnation.

Stifling the urge to lash out, Soraya withdrew into herself. What did she care if the Emir's lackey didn't approve of her? Even if, far from being a lackey he was one of the most powerful men in the country?

She had more on her mind than winning his approval. His news changed her life.

'Give me tomorrow,' she said, her voice husky with tension that threatened to choke her. 'Then I'll have a better idea.'

How long to pack her gear, say her goodbyes and, above all, get her research in some sort of order? She feared however long it took wouldn't be enough.

Anxiety welled and she beat it back. Time enough to give in to fear when she was alone. She refused to let this man see her weak.

Abruptly she stood. He rose too, dwarfing the booth and

crowding her space. Instantly she was transported to the club where his touch had sapped common sense. Where just for a moment she'd wanted to lean close to his powerful frame rather than escape his hold. Fear closed around her.

'I want to go home.' Even to her own ears her voice held a betraying wobble. Paris had become her home, a haven where she'd been able to spread her wings and enjoy a measure of freedom for the first time. The idea of returning to Bakhara, to marriage…

'I'll see you back.' Already he was ushering her through the café, one hand hovering near her elbow as if to ensure she didn't do a runner. He dropped payment on the counter where the waitress beamed her approval.

What was wrong with the girl? Couldn't she see he was the sort of bad-tempered, take-charge brute who'd make any woman's life a misery?

Clearly not. The waitress's gaze followed him longingly, needling Soraya's temper.

'Thank you but I can make my own way.'

To her chagrin he was already hailing a taxi—a miracle at this time of the morning. It was daylight but the city was just stirring. Before she could reiterate her point he was opening the door for her then climbing in the other side.

'I said—'

Her words disintegrated as he gave her address to the driver. Her heart thudded and she sank back in her corner.

Of course he knew her address. How else would he have located her? But the thought of Zahir El Hashem shouldering his way into her cosy flat sent disquiet scudding through her. Instinct warned her to keep her distance.

She didn't want him near her.

The fact that he sat as far from her as the wide back seat allowed should have pleased her. Instead it struck her as insulting. He didn't have to make such a conspicuous issue of keeping his distance, so grimly silent.

What she'd done to annoy him, she had no idea. *He* was the

one whose behaviour was questionable, following her every move in the nightclub. What was that about?

Fifteen minutes later they stood on the pavement before her building. He'd overridden her assurance that he needn't see her to the entrance, just as he'd paid the taxi fare as she fumbled for cash. Polite gestures no doubt but he insidiously invaded her space, encroaching on her claim to be an independent woman.

Never before had that claim seemed so precious.

Her heart plunged as she thought of what lay ahead.

A promise to keep.

A duty to perform.

A *lifetime* of it.

So much for the tantalising sense of freedom she'd only just found. The dreams she'd dared to harbour. She'd been mad to let herself imagine a future of her own making.

'Here. Thank you.' She tugged his jacket off her shoulders. Instantly she missed its heavy, comforting warmth and, she realised with horror, its subtle spicy scent. The scent of *him*.

She looked into his shadowed face, unable to read his expression. But there was no mistaking the care he took not to touch her as he took the jacket from her hands. As if she might contaminate him!

Why had she, even for a moment, worried what he thought of her? She'd long ago learned to rise above what others thought, what they expected. Only by being true to herself and those she cared for had she found strength.

'Goodbye. Thank you for seeing me home.' What did it matter if her voice was stilted with indignation? She inclined her head stiffly and turned, unlocking the door.

'It's no trouble.' His deep voice rumbled, low and soft as a zephyr of hot desert wind, across her nape. Too late she realised she *felt* his warm breath, a caress on her bare skin as she stepped into the foyer and he followed.

Soraya slammed to a halt and felt the heat of his big frame behind her. Static electricity sparked and rippled across her flesh. It dismayed her. She'd never known anything like it.

But, she rationalised, till tonight she'd never been so close to a man other than her father.

Would she feel this strange surge of power in the air and across her skin when she went to the Emir?

Despite the heat of Zahir's body Soraya shivered.

'I'll see you to your apartment.'

Flattening her lips at his assumption she couldn't look after herself in her own building, she strode across the foyer. No point arguing. She had as much chance of budging him as of moving the Eiffel Tower.

But she refused to share the miniscule lift. The thought of being cocooned with him in that cramped space sent a spasm of horror through her. She'd rather take the five flights of stairs, even if her new shoes *were* pinching.

Soraya was ridiculously breathless when she reached her floor. She shoved her key in the door and turned to face him.

He wasn't even breathing quickly after their rapid ascent. Nor did he feel that strange under-the-skin restlessness that so unnerved her. That was clear from his impassive face. He looked solid and immoveable. Nothing pierced his control.

'Here.' He held out a thick cream card. On one side was a mobile-phone number. No name, nothing else. On the other he'd scrawled in bold, slashing strokes the name of a hotel she knew by reputation only. 'Call me if you need anything. I'll make all the necessary arrangements.'

No point in assuring him again she'd do her own organizing; it would be a waste of breath. He had the look of a man who heard what he chose to hear. She'd sort out the details later when she wasn't so weary.

'Thank you,' she murmured, resolutely hauling her gaze from his clear-eyed stare. 'Good night.'

Behind her she pushed open the door to the apartment.

'Is that you, Soraya?' From inside, Lisle's husky voice shattered the stilted silence. 'We're in the bedroom. Come in and join us.'

A stifled noise made her look up. Zahir El Hashem looked

for once shaken out of his complacency. His eyes were wide and his mouth slack. He blinked and opened his mouth as if to speak but Soraya had had enough.

She stepped through the door and swung it closed. For the length of five heartbeats she stood, her back pressed against the door, waiting for his imperious summons, for there was no doubt he'd been about to speak.

Instead there was silence. Even through the door she sensed his presence, like a disapproving thundercloud. Her skin prickled as if she'd touched a live wire and her pulse pattered out of sync.

'Soraya? Julie's here too. Come on in.'

'Coming,' she croaked, knowing she had no hope of escaping Lisle or her sister. Julie must have stopped by to see how things were with her twin as soon as Lisle's boyfriend had left.

Girly gossip wasn't what Soraya needed but at least it would take her mind off the news she'd just received: that her wonderful adventure in Paris was over and she was returning home to fulfil the duty she'd been bound to from the age of fourteen. The duty she'd become accustomed to thinking was in some far-off future that became less real with every passing year.

Yet as she snicked the bolt shut and scooped up Lisle's carelessly discarded camisole, Soraya was surprised to realise it was Zahir El Hashem's strong features that filled her mind. Not those of her betrothed.

Zahir stared at the door, one hand still raised as if to stop it shutting. Or force it open.

Shock held him rigid. It wasn't a familiar feeling. He was a man of some experience. Little surprised him. To be at a loss because she'd been invited to make up a threesome with the lovers he'd seen last night should be impossible.

Yet he rocked back on his feet, his gut clenching as if he'd caught a hammer blow to the belly. Searing bile snaked through his system.

Despite what he'd seen earlier, he'd almost convinced himself he'd been mistaken about Soraya. That the woman who carried herself with such poise and grace, yet with that intriguing shadow of anxiety in her eyes, was special. When he'd relaxed his guard he'd liked her, despite his doubts.

Stupid wishful thinking!

Had she deliberately sidetracked him?

Valiantly he'd tried to keep his eyes off the syncopated sway of her pert backside as she climbed the stairs in precarious heels. Even when he'd managed not to look he'd imagined the slip of soft fabric across warm, rounded flesh. His palms had tingled with remembered heat.

Anger welled. His hands fisted and his jaw ached as he clenched his teeth against the need to bellow out her name.

She'd played him for a fool. Tried to con him.

He felt...gutted.

He slumped against the door, hand splayed against it for support, recalling that discarded scrap of lingerie casually discarded just inside the door.

He'd spoiled her fun at the club and, he realised now, with the news she had to return to Bakhara where her every move would be scrutinised. Was she even now hauling that slinky dress over her head to join her friends in a little early-morning debauchery?

Nausea writhed.

Breathing heavily, Zahir sought calm.

Could he have misread what he'd seen and heard? He had so little evidence. Was he wrong to assume the worst? It was tempting to hope so.

Till he realised how much he *wanted* to be wrong. Fear feathered his backbone as he registered the sense almost of longing within him.

From the first his instinct had screamed a warning about Soraya Karim: she was dangerous. She tested his control to the limit and messed with his judgement.

He couldn't let her undermine his duty too.

Zahir sighed and scrubbed his hand over gritty eyes, sud-

denly more tired than he could remember. How could he break
it to Hussein that the woman he planned to marry might not
be fit for the honour?

'I'm sorry, madam. I'm afraid the guest you enquired about
isn't available.'

'Not in or not available?' Soraya tamped down the steam-
ing anger that had been simmering for hours. 'It's important I
see him as soon as possible.'

'Excuse me a moment while I check.' The receptionist
turned to confer with a colleague, leaving Soraya free to focus
on her surroundings.

The foyer was luxurious in the bred-in-the-bone way you'd
expect of one of Paris's grandest hotels. From the crimson
carpet leading in from the cobblestoned pavement to the dis-
creetly helpful staff, exquisite antiques and massive Venetian
glass chandeliers, the placed screamed money, but in the most
hushed and refined tones. The guests, whether wearing couture, business suits or staggeringly mismatched casuals, took
the opulence in their stride, as only the super-wealthy could.

Soraya in her workaday jeans, T-shirt and loose jacket
had never felt so out of place. Her family, one of the oldest in
Bakhara, was comfortably off but had never aspired to this
sort of rarefied luxury.

Even her shoes, her one pretension to elegance, had been
snaffled in a miraculous end-of-sale bargain.

She stood taller. None of that mattered. All that mattered
was seeing *him*. A tremor of repressed fury skated down her
spine. Hadn't he promised her a day to get her bearings and
then contact him? He'd had no right…

'I'm sorry for the delay, madam.' The receptionist was back.
'I'm able to tell you the guest you asked for has left strict instructions not to be disturbed.'

Soraya's lips compressed. That was why he hadn't answered
his phone for the past two hours and she'd finally had to leave

her work and come here in person. As if she didn't have more important things to concern her!

Why give her his phone number if he was going to be in-communicado for hours?

An image flashed into her brain of the waitress at the café melting at the sight of his blatant masculinity.

Was that why he couldn't be disturbed? Some assignation with an adoring woman?

'Thank you.' Her voice was crisp. 'In that case I'll wait till he *is* available.'

With a humph of disgust, Soraya stepped away from the desk.

Zahir El Hashem would soon discover she was no pushover.

In the early hours of this morning she'd been numb with the shock of his news, so dizzy with it she'd let him take charge. Now she'd had time to absorb the fact that she had no choice but to face her future head-on. That didn't stop the regrets, the anxiety, the downright fear. But she had to be strong if she was to survive the ordeal ahead. At the moment that meant teaching Zahir she wasn't some lackey to be ordered about at his convenience.

She was, like it or not, his Emir's future queen and a woman in her own right.

Soraya stalked across the room, oblivious now to its refined opulence, and plonked herself down on a plump sofa. She un-zipped her laptop case and switched on the computer.

She'd rather be angry than fearful. And better than either was to immerse herself in something she really cared about. Two minutes later she was focused on her report, seeking an elusive error in the heat-transfer calculations.

Soraya didn't know what finally tugged her attention from the latest projections, but something made her look up, a sixth sense that sliced through her absorption.

A cluster of men in dark suits stood on the far side of the lobby. She recognised one as a senior French politician, his face familiar from news reports. But it was the tallest of the group who drew her frowning attention. His skin was burnished a dark honey gold, his features arresting.

Abruptly he looked up, his eyes locking instantly with hers. Shock danced down her spine at the impact.

Just like before.

The world had fallen away when he'd looked at her last night too.

Her hands jerked on the laptop keys. From the corner of her vision she saw a stream of extra rows appear in the carefully constructed table of technical analysis. Yet she couldn't drag her eyes from his.

In leather and denim he'd been a virile bad boy with an undeniable aura of danger.

Today, in exquisite tailoring and with an air of urbane assurance, he looked like he'd stepped from the ranks of the world's power brokers.

Who *was* Zahir El Hashem? Politician or heavy? Sophisticate or rogue?

Why did locking eyes with him make Soraya's heart thud to a discordant beat that stirred unfamiliar sensations?

She jerked her gaze away, blindly hit 'save' on her document and fumbled to shut down the laptop.

She'd had no sleep and she was stressed; no wonder she imagined things. There'd been no instantaneous pulse of connection between them. She'd simply imagined its heavy weight constricting her lungs and drawing her belly tight.

Shoving her laptop into its case she looked up to see him striding towards her.

Trepidation struck her. An awareness that, despite his elegant apparel and their rarefied surroundings, there was an elemental toughness about him she'd do well to remember. Only last night she'd recognised the desert warrior in him. Now as he approached Soraya knew she hadn't imagined the subtle scent of danger clinging to him.

'What's wrong? Why are you here?' His low voice drew the

fine hairs on her nape to prickling attention even as dark heat pooled low inside. It only fuelled her anger.

She refused to feel fear…or anything else for him.

'To see you, of course,' she hissed, jerking to her feet and wishing she was taller so he couldn't loom quite so effectively over her.

His narrowed eyes surveyed the room quickly and comprehensively. It was the sort of look she'd seen bodyguards use, searching for threat.

She'd give him threat!

'We had an agreement.' This time she kept her voice low and even. 'You broke it.'

His dark eyebrows climbed high but he gave no other reaction. 'Come.' He gestured for her to precede him.

Instantly Soraya shifted her weight, widening her stance a fraction as if to plant herself more firmly. She had no intention of meekly following him anywhere.

'I think not. We can talk here.'

Something flickered in those deeply hooded eyes. Something that might have been surprise or annoyance. Frankly, she didn't care. Instinct told her not to be alone with him. She knew next to nothing about him and looking at that granite-carved jaw, she wouldn't put it past him to try coercion.

'This is not the place for our conversation. This is a delicate matter and the person I represent—'

'Would perfectly understand my preference for meeting you here, rather than in a private room.'

He said nothing, just surveyed her with a look that was impossible to interpret. A look that seemed to take in everything from her too-fast breathing to the laptop she clutched like a shield to her chest.

Finally he nodded. 'Of course. If that is what you wish.' He turned and indicated a couple of chairs grouped at the rear of the room. 'Though perhaps we could go some place where we're less likely to be overheard.'

He had a point. Soraya nodded stiffly and let him usher her across the room.

Zahir frowned as he followed her. That instant surge of adrenalin in his blood, the momentary fear that something was wrong, had undermined his calm. All because she'd come looking for him when it was the last thing he'd expected.

It was absurd. Clearly she was in no danger. Panic was a weakness he didn't indulge in. Yet his pulse thundered in his ears as he watched her thread her way across the room.

He didn't like her, didn't approve of her, so why the instant, gut-deep need to protect that had made him hurry to her? He wanted to put it down to duty honed by years of training, but it wasn't that. From the first she'd stirred instincts and feelings that discomfited him. However much he fought it he felt... connected to her. Ever since that first, blinding moment of recognition.

She settled on a gilded sofa and made a production of crossing those long legs. As he seated himself opposite her, Zahir forced his gaze from the way the soft denim clung to each dip and curve.

'You wanted to see me?'

'Not really, but I had little choice.' Her neat white teeth snapped off each word. 'You weren't answering your phone.'

Ah. That was why she was in a temper. When she'd wrecked his plans to return to Bakhara today he'd used the extra time to fit in some meetings. Clearly she expected him to be at her beck and call like some underling.

'As you saw, I had business to conduct.' He refused to apologise for not being available at her whim. 'How can I assist you?'

Her eyes flashed ebony fire. 'By keeping your word.'

Zahir stiffened. 'That is not in question.' Did she have any concept of the insult she offered him?

'Isn't it?' She leaned forward and her scent insinuated itself into his nostrils. Light and delicate, like a field of mountain flowers awakening to the day's first sun. It had haunted him all day, a sense memory he'd tried to forget. 'We agreed you'd give me today to get organised yet my flatmate rang me at five this afternoon because a team of removalists had turned up wanting to pack my belongings.'

Zahir settled back in his seat and inclined his head. 'We agreed that you'd have today. We also agreed that I'd take care of the arrangements. I've done so. You've had your day to organise yourself.'

Colour mounted her cheeks and her eyes glittered with temper. Women could be so predictable when they didn't get what they wanted. He waited for a blast of ungoverned rage.

It didn't come.

Instead she sat back against the silk brocade of her seat.

'You don't approve of me, do you?' Her voice was coolly measured. 'Is that what this is about? Is that why you're being so high-handed?'

Momentarily he was thrown by her directness. He encountered it so rarely since he'd moved into the diplomatic sphere. It was the sort of tactic he used himself to great effect when others preferred to circle the truth. Cutting through the niceties to the heart of the matter was sometimes the most effective way forward.

He hadn't expected it from her.

Unwilling admiration stirred.

'My opinion of you is not in question, Ms Karim. My role is simply to facilitate your safe arrival to Bakhara.'

'Don't give me that! You're more than a courier.' She nodded to where he'd stood saying farewell to his guests. 'That's clear from the leaders who came here to meet you. You're trying to railroad me for your own reasons.'

She was clever too. Obviously she'd recognised the man tipped to become the next French foreign minister.

But what disturbed him was her accusation he was pushing her to hurry because it suited him.

He should have contacted Hussein this morning and voiced his concerns about Soraya Karim. But he'd baulked at the notion. That sort of conversation had to take place man-to-man, not long distance. It had the added advantage that Zahir could then walk away from her and concentrate on the work he'd been preparing for all his life.

'What is it about Paris that keeps you delaying? What's more important than your promise to marry?'

The colour faded from her cheeks and for a second he saw something flicker in the rich depths of her pansy-dark eyes. Something that looked like genuine pain. It surprised him for it seemed at odds with his image of a selfish pleasure-seeking woman.

'I have things to wrap up before I go.'

Things or relationships? His jaw tightened.

'Surely it won't take more than a day to say goodbye to your special *friends*.' He nodded curtly to her laptop. 'And no doubt you'll stay in contact.' Was she the sort who suffered withdrawal if disconnected from social media?

Her smooth forehead puckered then she shrugged. 'I have some work to finish too.'

Soraya almost laughed aloud as a flash of disbelief widened his eyes. Clearly he thought her some dilettante who used university as an excuse for a holiday in Paris.

He recovered quickly. 'It's summer. University break.'

'Have you heard of summer school? Between semesters?'

'I applaud your diligence.' But his tone belied his words. 'Are you saying you have to be here to complete your work? Surely alternative arrangements can be made?'

Circumstances being the fact that she was expected to return home meekly and marry a man, a virtual stranger, more than thirty years her senior.

Cold wrapped itself around Soraya's chest and seeped into bones that seemed suddenly brittle and aged. She drew a deep breath, willing away the panic that threatened whenever she thought too far ahead.

That was the problem; she'd forgotten to think ahead. For too long she'd assumed the future was nebulous and unreal. From the moment at fourteen, when her father had explained the honour bestowed on their family by the Emir's interest in her, through every year when Emir Hussein had remained a distant yet benign figure.

At fourteen the betrothal had been exciting, like something from an age-old tale. Later it had grown less and less real, especially when her fiancé had shown little interest beyond polite responses to her father's updates on her wellbeing and educational progress.

Now it was suddenly all too real.

'It's not just the work,' she blurted out. 'I'd planned to be here longer and I want to make the most of my time in France.'

'I'm sure you're doing just that.' His lips twisted.

She ignored his disapproval. 'I can finish up some of my work elsewhere, but not all of it.' She gestured to the laptop. 'Besides, I don't want a direct flight to Bakhara.'

His only response was to lift his eyebrows, stoking her impatience.

'I intend to travel overland. In all these months I haven't been out of Paris and I want to see more of the country before I return.'

And store up some precious memories—of her last days of freedom. It wasn't too much to ask. Once she returned she'd be the woman the Emir and his people expected. She'd marry a man renowned for his devotion to duty and her life would be circumscribed by that.

She needed this time, just a little time, to adjust to the fact that her life as an individual was ending. The alternative, to return immediately, stifled the breath in her lungs and sent panic shuddering through her.

'That's not possible. The Emir is expecting you.'

She nodded, glad now that she'd found the courage to do what she'd never done before and call the Bakhari Palace, giving her name and asking for the Emir. It had been surprisingly easy.

'Yes, he is.' For the first time she smiled. 'I spoke to him today. He thinks it's a wonderful idea that I take my time and soak up some of the sights along the way. He agrees it will be educational for me to get a better understanding of other places and people, not just Paris.'

It had felt odd talking to the man who for so long had been a distant figure and who soon would be her husband.

Zahir's stunned expression would have pleased her if she'd wanted to score points off this man who always seemed so sure of himself. But she had more important concerns.

'I've got till the end of the month.' That would give her the breathing space she so desperately needed. There was only one problem, but right now it should be the least of her worries. She squared her shoulders and met his eyes. 'The Emir's only stipulation was that you accompany me.'

CHAPTER FOUR

'I KNOW it's not what you planned, Zahir, but I see huge benefits in this trip. Soraya was very convincing.'

Zahir gritted his teeth. He just bet she had been. He heard the smile in Hussein's tone even over the phone. No doubt she'd employed her soft, sultry voice to best advantage in her long-distance call to Bakhara.

'But a week is more than enough, isn't it? The sooner she returns the better, surely?'

'It will be a big change for her,' Hussein answered slowly. 'Living as my wife in the palace. Meeting VIPs, playing a role in diplomatic functions. Plus there's the work that will be expected of her with our own people. She'll be an advocate for many who, for whatever reason, are daunted by approaching their ruler directly. Giving her a chance to mix with as wide a range of people as possible can only be an advantage.'

He paused. 'That's one of the reasons I supported her studying in Paris. She needs to broaden her horizons, ready for her future role.'

Zahir stared unseeingly at the lights of Paris. His heart sank. Not just because Hussein supported Soraya's plan to delay her return. Far worse was the burden of suspicion she wasn't fit to be his mentor's bride.

He thrust a hand through his hair. How could he disabuse Hussein?

How could he not?

He'd do anything to save Hussein pain. The older man was more than a father to him. Friend, mentor, hero, he'd shown Zahir care, regard and even love when no one else had. He'd brought him up more like a son than a charity case. A not-quite-orphan shouldn't have warranted the Emir's personal attention.

Zahir owed him everything: his place in the world, his education, his self-respect, even his life.

He was caught between shattering Hussein's illusions about his bride and letting her dupe him.

His belly churned. 'Hussein, I—'

'I know you're disappointed, Zahir. You're eager to take up the post of provincial governor.'

A sliver of guilt carved its way through Zahir's gut. 'You know me too well.'

Hussein's chuckle was like the man himself, warm and compelling. 'How could I not? You're the son I never had.'

Something rose in Zahir's chest, a welling sensation that tightened his lungs and choked his vocal chords. Despite their closeness, the regard between him and Hussein was rarely spoken. Bakhari males left emotion to their womenfolk, focusing instead on masculine concerns such as pride, duty and honour.

'You make it sound like your time has past. You're in your late fifties, not your dotage. You've got plenty of time to father a son. A whole family.'

And, with a young, sexy bride, nothing was more likely.

Out of nowhere Zahir glimpsed an image of Hussein holding Soraya close, pulling her to him and letting his hands slip over the curve of her hip, the soft fabric of her dress enhancing the femininity of her shapely figure.

He swallowed hard as a jagged spike of pain skewered him. His breath shallowed and he turned to stride down the length of the suite, fighting sudden nausea.

He was tired of being cooped up. He longed for the clean air of the desert, the wide sky studded with diamond-bright stars. *The total absence of Soraya Karim.*

'Well, time will tell,' was all Hussein said. 'But as for the governorship…'

'That doesn't matter.' Zahir splayed a hand against one wall and stared out at the glittering spectacle of the Eiffel Tower sparkling with a million electric lights. He'd trade it in a second for the light of the moon over the desert, highlighting dunes and silhouetting proud, ancient citadels.

'Of course it matters. You'll be the best governor the place has had.'

Silence engulfed them. No doubt Hussein, like himself, was remembering the long period when Bakhara's largest province had been ruled by a ruthless, decadent and utterly unscrupulous tribal leader. A man who'd tried many years before to increase his prestige by backing a coup to unseat Hussein.

Zahir's father.

His biological father, never his *real* father.

It sickened Zahir that he shared the blood of a traitor, a man who'd clung to his position only because of Hussein's forgiveness and the fact that removing him would have caused more unrest at a dangerous, volatile time.

'Your faith in me means everything.' Zahir bowed his head. It was the closest he'd ever come to expressing aloud his devotion to the man who'd rescued him, ragged, neglected and virtually feral at the age of four from his father's palace.

Rather than speak it, Zahir had spent a lifetime demonstrating his loyalty, his regard, his love.

'As does yours, Zahir.' Hussein's tone held a husky warmth that spoke far more than words. 'As for the governorship—it will be there waiting for you. I think my bride isn't the only one who'll benefit from a break. You've pushed yourself hard lately. Take your time and relax. Who knows?' He chortled. 'You might even enjoy the novelty of a vacation.'

Zahir opened his mouth to say he didn't need a vacation. He thrived on responsibility, challenge, pressure. The prospect of managing the vast province held an allure he couldn't put in words. To have total responsibility, rather than be another's aide: it had captured his interest from the moment Hussein had broached it.

'It's not simply the time away.' Zahir paused, wondering how to continue. He wasn't used to being at a loss for words.

'Go on.'

He drew a difficult breath and wished his concerns were about something as simple as the next bilateral trade agreement or progress on a major public-works programme.

'Your fiancée. She's not what I expected.'

Silence. Zahir knew Hussein valued his opinion on so many difficult issues. He'd even trusted him with his life. But this was different.

'I see.'

Zahir shook his head. Hussein *didn't* see. That was the problem. He'd left Soraya to her own devices in Paris, believing she was worthy of his trust.

'I'm not sure she's…quite the woman you expect.'

'Taken you by surprise, has she?' Hussein's chuckle was rich.

Zahir's hand clenched in a taut fist. 'You could say that.' No, he mustn't hide the truth any longer. 'I'm afraid she may not be the right woman for you.'

Hell! He'd give anything not to have to break this news. Hussein deserved better, so much better than a party girl who shared her sexual favours freely.

'Your concern does you credit, Zahir. But I know more of Soraya than you think. I know she's exactly the woman I need.' When he spoke again his words silenced Zahir's protests. 'We will talk on your return. In the meantime, know that I believe in her as I believe in you, Zahir. I trust you both.'

'What are you doing here?' The words shot out of Soraya's mouth before she could stop them. She wasn't used to opening her door to find six-foot-something of male leaning indolently against the doorjamb.

Her heart leapt up against her throat and she felt light-headed at the impact of him.

He was so close she recognised the clean, spicy scent of his skin. It reminded her of the strange sensations she'd experienced when he'd held her in his arms and she'd felt...

'Good morning, Soraya. It's good to see you looking well.' He straightened but only so he could loom imposingly.

'How did you get into the building?' She sounded absurdly breathless given the fact she'd expected to meet him downstairs in ten minutes. But, she was learning that meeting this man head-on was marginally easier if one was prepared.

His gaze raked her face. Heat combusted and spread under her skin.

Who was she kidding? There was nothing easy about this. She only wished she understood what it was about him that screwed her tension up to such dangerous levels.

He shrugged and she couldn't help but follow the movement of his broad shoulders beneath the pale, exquisitely laundered shirt. Casual, expensive elegance; that was the theme of the day. Scrupulously shaved jaw and a heavy yet discreet watch she was sure she recognised from one of Lisle's fashion magazines.

'One of the tenants let me in when she saw me waiting outside.' His glimmer of a smile drew the tightness in her belly even harder.

Soraya breathed deep. Of course it had been a woman. Had she taken one look at Zahir's compelling face and melted deep inside the way Soraya had in the nightclub?

She stiffened her spine.

'I'd expected to meet you at the car.'

'And I thought you might appreciate help with your luggage.' The hint of a smile had vanished and his eyes held that hard glitter she knew masked disapproval.

She forced down the churlish impulse to refuse. The way he took control so smoothly exacerbated her deepest fears about giving up her independence, reminding her that, once married, she would be bound to honour and, above all, obey. She repressed a quiver of apprehension and looked away.

'Thank you. That's very kind.' She stepped aside and invited him in.

'No farewell party?' He looked past her to the neat sitting room and the small, empty corridor.

'No.' She'd said her goodbyes earlier. Parting with Lisle in particular had been difficult. She'd had no intention of doing that under Zahir's assessing gaze.

Despite their different backgrounds, Soraya and Lisle had forged far more than a casual friendship. For the first time Soraya had glimpsed what it might be like to have a sister. Outgoing where Soraya was reserved, flamboyant rather than contained, funny, warm and impulsive—Lisle had been a revelation to a woman who'd spent her life in cloistered, sedate, correct social circles. Lisle was a whirlwind, ripping into Soraya's quiet life and setting it on a new path. One that had opened her eyes to all the world could offer a woman with her life ahead of her.

Except that now those possibilities crumbled to nothing. Soraya's future was set, had been since she was fourteen. It was too late to change it now.

'Soraya?'

She blinked and looked up to find him closer. For a split second she'd have said she read concern in his hooded eyes. She blinked again and the mirage was gone.

'Here.' She gestured to the case behind her in the hallway.

'That's all?' He looked past her as if to locate a secret stash of luggage.

'That's all. Your removalists were very efficient. My books and other bits and pieces are already on their way to Bakhara.' Her voice dropped to a husky note. She really had to pull herself together.

Despite the claustrophobic sense of the future smothering her, she knew the man she'd agreed to marry had reputedly been a devoted husband to his now-dead first wife. He was decent, generous and honourable.

That was more than many women could say.

It would have to be enough. It wasn't as if she was eager to seek out love. She knew what a devastating emotion that was.

As for her tentative dreams—instead she'd have to put her energies into the goals that had enticed her when she had been a starry-eyed teen: being a queen who made a real difference to her people. Being a good wife. At least with her qualifications she could be the former.

'I'll just get my shoulder bag.'

Thirty seconds later she was in her room, hugging close the oversized bag she'd haggled for in the markets two weeks ago. Only it wasn't her room any more. Stripped of her possessions, it was an empty shell. Not the place she'd been so happy.

Stupid to be sentimental about it.

There was no point dwelling on what was past. She'd learned that as a child, bereft and confused.

She turned and found Zahir in the doorway, his gaze, as ever, fixed on her. A subterranean tremor quaked through her, threatening to destabilise the control she fought so valiantly to maintain.

Turning quickly, she scooped up her laptop.

'I'm ready.'

The Loire River snaked below them like a bright pewter ribbon. Studded along its banks and beyond were neat towns, a patchwork of farms and a scattering of chateaux.

But Zahir's attention wasn't on the view, even when the chopper swooped low over quaint towns or stately homes.

It was the woman next to him who riveted Zahir's thoughts and his gaze. Uptight from the moment he turned up at her door, she'd grown coolly distant when he'd informed her they wouldn't travel by car as she'd planned.

She seemed to think he'd countermanded the idea out of a need to take control!

He huffed silently to himself. He had no need to prove his authority.

What he had was a burning need *not* to be cooped up alone with Soraya for the time it would take to drive to their destination.

Zahir couldn't pinpoint what it was about her that made him edgy—it was more than his qualms about her unsuitability as Hussein's bride.

Yet as they headed south-west from Paris he hadn't been able to drag his attention from her. He'd read her initial nerves, watched as she gradually relaxed and began to talk with the pilot. Initially dour, the pilot now chatted easily, flattered no doubt by her questions on everything from pilot training to wind speed and the local topography.

She was a woman who could charm a man with ease.

'You're enjoying the trip?' Zahir found himself asking. He suppressed the suspicion that he'd spoken only to break the camaraderie building between the other two.

'Absolutely.' There was a breathy quality to her voice that told him she was smiling even though she faced away, peering at the view. 'I love seeing everything laid out like this. It's fantastic.'

'I'm glad you like it.'

'Thank you for organising it.' She swung round and the pleasure on her face arrested him. It lit her from within, making her eyes glow and her face come alive.

Something inside Zahir shuddered into being: a recognition, a sense almost of rightness, he couldn't explain.

He'd seen her angry, defiant, exhausted. He'd seen her furious and frigidly cool but, he realised, he'd never seen her happy.

Maybe it would have been better to travel by car after all. *Safer.*

'You've never been in a helicopter before?' It was easier to talk than dwell on the impact of that knockout grin.

She shook her head and a tendril of dark hair slipped free of the knot at the back of her head and coiled down past her breast.

Involuntarily his fingers twitched, as if needing to feel its softness.

The preternatural feeling of recognition grew to something like déjà vu: as if Zahir had been with her before, had watched her joyous smile and felt that deep-down explosion of blistering heat. He could envisage her pulling her hair free of its pins so it swung in a seductive silk curtain, inviting his touch.

'No, I've never flown in a helicopter before. Isn't it terrific? I love the feeling when we swoop low then rise up high again.'

On cue the pilot angled the chopper down to circle a bluff crowned by a half-ruined tower then lifted them back up.

A throaty gurgle escaped her lips. 'Like that. Thanks, Marc.'

The pilot nodded silently and Zahir knew a moment's searing discomfort. As if the easy friendliness between the two had the power to annoy him.

The notion was absurd.

'I can't wait to try it again. I've decided I like air travel after all.' She turned away to watch as they passed over a field of sunflowers, head bent as if utterly absorbed.

'You didn't enjoy it before?'

'My only other flight was on the jet from Bakhara to Paris, so I couldn't be sure.'

Zahir sat back in his seat, processing that. 'You'd never been on a flight before then?' He'd imagined her spending holidays at foreign resorts then shopping till she dropped in the expensive boutiques of various capital cities.

She shook her head and he watched, transfixed by the wistful smile that shaped her face as she half-turned. 'I'd never been out of Bakhara before.'

No wonder Hussein had seen benefit in her studying abroad. No wonder he thought exposure to other places and people would do her good.

Bakhara was no longer the feudal state it had been till recently. The wife of the country's ruler would need polish, poise and some exposure to the wider world.

A pity her exposure hadn't been more carefully supervised.

Zahir frowned. Had she been wild for the hedonistic plea-sures Paris offered or had she been seduced by them? He remembered the husky voice inviting her to bed the other morn-ing, and the blatant lust in that pseudo-intellectual's face at the club. There'd be no shortage of people eager to introduce Soraya to life's seamier pleasures.

Heat trickled through his belly. What had Hussein been thinking, letting her loose in Paris without a chaperone? Without someone to guide and protect her, had she been easy prey?

Yet, even as he thought it, Zahir *knew* he was wrong. Soraya Karim was no easy victim. Beneath the feminine sway of hips and that delicious pout of a mouth was a will of iron. Look at how she'd managed to get her own way over delaying her re-turn to Bakhara. Whatever she'd done, she'd done with her eyes wide-open.

The heat in his gut twisted in a sickening swirl.

He vowed he at least wouldn't succumb to her blandish-ments.

Ahead Soraya glimpsed spires amidst a dark swathe of green. As they approached, her breath hitched at the sheer fairy-tale beauty of the chateau below them. Pale grey, almost white in the bright sunlight, it boasted an abundance of tow-ers capped with conical slate roofs. The windows were large and mullioned, reflecting the sun glinting off the moat that surrounded it. An arched bridge led across to vast lawns and ornamental gardens. The whole was enclosed by a forest that isolated it from everything else. Like an enchanted world.

She sighed. It was so beautiful, so different from anything she'd seen either in Paris or at home. No wonder Lisle had told her she couldn't miss the Loire Valley! She'd said it would ap-peal to the dreamer in her.

Just the place for Prince Charming to appear and spirit her away on his milk-white stallion.

Her smile twisted. She wasn't in the market for a rescuing

prince. She'd never yearned for romance, not after weathering the destructive aftermath of her parents' disastrous love match.

Besides, one prince was enough in any girl's life.

More than enough.

She wrapped her arms around herself as a chill invaded her bones.

Try as she might, nothing could take her mind off the fact that in a few short weeks she'd be at the Emir's court, preparing for her wedding—to give herself to a stranger.

Dread carved a hollow in her chest, leaving a yawning hole where she'd once nurtured fledgling dreams. Not earth-shattering dreams, just the chance to make her own choices. To build a career she loved and live as she chose.

Right now they seemed as likely as flying to the moon.

It was only as the thud of the helicopter's rotors died that she realised they'd landed. Bewildered, she looked out to see they were between the forest and the river. In front of them rose the exquisite chateau she'd admired from the air.

Soraya tried to dredge up her enthusiasm for the fanciful architecture, the elegant embellishments, the beautiful symmetry. But the cold, hard fact of her looming future marred her appreciation.

She fumbled for her seatbelt, annoyed with herself. She should be making the most of every moment, of each new place and experience. Yet here she was doing what she'd vowed not to do—dwelling on what she couldn't change.

'Let me.' Zahir's warm fingers tangled with hers and she stiffened.

There had to be a scientific explanation for the pulse of energy that sparked under her skin whenever he touched her. Once it had been surprising—twice, too much of a coincidence. Now she found it…disturbing.

'Thank you.' She scrambled out of the door before he could come around and help. Her knees felt ridiculously weak but she put that down to the after-effects of her first chopper flight.

She went forward to thank Marc. He'd been friendly and so patient with her questions.

She'd barely thanked him when Zahir loomed beside her.

'This way.' He didn't touch her again but with him so close she found herself cutting short her goodbyes and preceding him to the chateau.

'I think you'll like this,' he said as they crunched up the white gravel path. 'There's swimming, tennis, archery, riding—all the usual—and the restaurant has a couple of Michelin stars, of course.'

Of course.

'The day spa is renowned and you have a reservation there in—' he glanced at his watch '—forty minutes.'

Soraya shifted her stare from the opulent chateau to the man striding at her side.

'We're staying *here*?' She'd thought they'd stopped to get a better look since she'd wanted to visit the region.

'You don't approve?' He slashed a sideways glance at her then away, never slowing his pace. The set of his shoulders and the clench of his solid jaw spoke of impatience. Or was it anger?

From the very first, disapproval had emanated from him in waves. She was tired of it.

Soraya shook her head. 'No, it's not that.' She just wasn't accustomed to such grandeur; it made her uncomfortable. But, she reminded herself, she'd have to get used to it soon. The Emir of Bakhara was one of the wealthiest men in the world. 'I'm sure it will be…lovely.'

Zahir must have picked up her cautious tone for he stopped, blocking her path. 'If you have a problem, tell me.' His eyes iced over, chilling her anew. 'I'd rather know now than have you running to the Emir and bothering him with your complaints when he's busy.'

Soraya's head jerked back as if he'd slapped her.

The Emir hadn't minded her calling. In fact, he'd sounded pleased she'd rung and surprisingly delighted with her plan for a slow route home.

Nor had she any need to explain herself to Zahir El Hashem. Whatever it was that twisted him in knots wasn't her concern.

She met his glacial stare with what she hoped was casual disdain. 'As you pointed out a few days ago, the Emir is my future husband. I will call him if I wish.'

No need to say she had no intention of making further calls. She refused to let the man looming like a thundercloud think he could bully her. She stepped forward, intending to brush by him, but he didn't budge, just stood before her, blocking her way—unless she chose to scramble through the rose bushes edging the path. He seemed all solid muscle and bone—broad enough to blot out the chateau with those shoulders and towering over her even though she wore her heels.

'One thing you should know.' His voice was soft, a low, lethal growl that sent primitive fear scudding down her spine. 'You betray him and you answer to me.'

Soraya's head shot up, her eyes clashing with his.

Gone was the coolness, the icy detachment. He was all heat and fury. She felt it sizzle around her like a force-field, drawing her in, trapping her. The air between them zapped and crackled with the emotion radiating from him.

For the first time Soraya saw *him*—not the polished, unreadable veneer of a man who hid his true thoughts behind impenetrable barriers.

She'd wondered what lay behind that façade. Now she had a glimpse and was stunned by what she discovered.

For all his appearance of detachment, and despite his reputation as a diplomatic trouble shooter, Zahir El Hashem was a man of passion and volcanic temper. He *cared* about the Emir, and not just as the man who paid his salary.

Prickles of heat broke out across her flesh as she met his glare and refused to back away.

'Your sentiment does you proud,' she said when finally she found her voice. 'But your judgement is seriously flawed if you think I intend to betray him.'

That was just it. She wasn't the sort to blithely walk away from a promise, even a promise given so young.

Her past had moulded her into a woman who understood the value of honour. And the destructive force of betrayal. Besides, she couldn't disappoint her father, who saw this as her bright, wonderful future. Nor could she betray the Emir, the man who'd given her back what she'd almost lost. She owed him so much.

No matter which way she looked at it, she was shackled to her destiny.

'Now,' she continued, her voice husky with weariness, 'please step out of my way. I want to go to my room.'

CHAPTER FIVE

IT WASN'T guilt Zahir felt.

He'd been right to warn her. Let her know he was watching her. That he had Hussein's back covered.

Zahir had willingly put himself between Hussein and danger in the past. It was what he'd trained to do. What he was proud to do. Dealing with an unfaithful woman was nothing compared to facing down a would-be assassin.

Yet something niggled at him. Something was *wrong*.

Gut instinct warned he'd missed something. That he didn't have the full picture—till he reminded himself he wasn't the sort to be swayed by a show of bravado and a flicker of pain in eyes like bruised pansies.

Yet he found himself pushing open the door to the hotel's plush day spa. It reeked of perfume, hothouse orchids and flushed female flesh.

'Can I help you, *monsieur*?' A pretty redhead looked up from the reception desk.

'Yes, I'm looking for Mademoiselle Karim.'

'Karim?' The woman frowned and turned to her computer. 'Ah, I thought I recognised the name. That booking was cancelled this morning.'

'Cancelled?' He'd made no such cancellation.

The redhead nodded. 'That's right. Mademoiselle rang from her room. She'd changed her mind and…' She looked up to find the plate-glass door to the spa swinging closed.

Twenty minutes later Zahir was on the road. At least he knew he wasn't chasing a runaway; her luggage was in her suite. Even her beloved laptop.

Only Soraya was missing.

He cursed himself and accelerated too soon out of a sweeping bend in the road.

How had he let her slip away? Why hadn't he confirmed she was set for a day's pampering rather than assuming it, before settling down with his own laptop?

Because he'd been too eager to put distance between them.

Whether pensive or defiant or giving him the cold shoulder, Soraya Karim tugged at something hot and hungry deep inside him.

Something he had no business feeling for the woman who, rightly or wrongly, was to marry Hussein.

That was the hell of it.

Why her?

He had his choice of women now he was *someone*. His mouth twisted in a smile of derision, remembering his youth, when lack of status had lost him the woman he'd fallen for so desperately. He'd thought his heart broken.

Of course he'd survived. As for his heart—he harboured no fantasies now about love. He never let women close to him emotionally. They barely caused a ripple in his life.

Until Soraya Karim.

Tension crawled through him. He'd had to force himself to give her space. Had he provided her with an opportunity to take off and meet a lover?

His only clues were the details of the car the concierge had organised for her and the map he'd provided—a map on which he'd marked the places Soraya had queried: a couple of chateaux, an old house and what turned out to be a nuclear power-plant. That last had to be a mistake. He mentally crossed it off his list and accelerated down a straight stretch of road, his mouth set.

* * *

It was late when he tracked her down.

A familiar, husky voice caught Zahir's ear. He slammed to a halt at the base of the stone stairs in the old house-cum-museum. Swinging his head round, he saw her.

She was safe.

Relief hit him so hard his knees weakened for a moment. An instant later fury descended, swirling through him like a desert storm.

Hussein trusted him to keep her safe yet he'd let her slip away. For the first time ever Zahir had let emotion interfere with his judgement, with his duty.

Inevitably she was talking with a man, her head bent close.

Zahir pushed away from the stairs, outrage pounding through him that he'd let himself worry about her. Then his mind processed what he saw and he stopped again, frowning.

This was no assignation. The man had stooped shoulders and greying hair. Beside him was a trim woman in her late sixties, smiling benignly as Soraya and her male companion discussed…mechanical gears?

Zahir moved to one side and saw what fixed their attention—a display of machinery. His frown deepened as he flashed a glance around the cellar of the old house.

All around were models of half-familiar machines. A whirli-gig that looked like the precursor to a helicopter. A model of a tilting bridge. A contraption for hauling water uphill by turn-ing a huge screw.

It hit Zahir then that he'd been right: he *didn't* understand Soraya. He'd missed something vital.

He intended to find out what it was.

'Ah, we mustn't keep you any longer. Thank you for your time, my dear. I've enjoyed our chat.' There was a twinkle in the old man's eyes as he looked past her and up.

Soraya's nape prickled and the hairs on her arms rose as if someone had walked over her grave.

Slowly she turned. Her gaze hit a broad chest in a snowy

shirt then climbed past a strong, sun-burnished throat to a familiar, rock-hard jaw, firm, sculpted lips, lean cheeks and eyes
of dazzling emerald.

Heat snaked from her chest to her abdomen, circling there
as he held her eyes.

'Hello, Soraya. You take some tracking down.'

Behind her she was aware of the older couple moving away
and knew regret. She'd so enjoyed their discussion. Now her
day of freedom was over. Was it imagination or did the sunlight dim, as if obscured by sudden cloud?

'Then why did you bother? I'm perfectly capable of looking
after myself.' Anger bit deep that she'd not been allowed even
a day of freedom. Was this what it would be like in Bakhara?
No time to herself? Always watched? Silently she railed against
the future she couldn't change.

'So I'm discovering.' Instead of the scowl she anticipated
she read only curiosity in his gaze. 'Shall we?' He gestured
towards the door that led into the garden.

Reluctantly she led the way. There was no point continuing
with her plans to see the rest of the estate now he was here. He'd
have some reason why she had to return to the chateau-hotel.

Choosing a seat at a shaded courtyard table, Soraya slipped
her sunglasses on. She needed all the protection she could get
against his piercing scrutiny.

Zahir didn't say anything, simply ordered iced water and
coffee then lounged, one arm slung along the back of his chair
as if totally relaxed, watching her.

Soraya's blood tingled in response to that look.

It was almost a relief when their order came. Surely now
he'd break the brooding suspense to berate her for leaving and
not telling him her plans?

She stiffened her spine in readiness and lifted her glass of
chilled water.

'Tell me about yourself,' he said at last, and her hand jerked
so she almost spilled the drink down her dress. It was the last
thing she'd expected him to say.

'Why?' Sourness tinged her response. 'I'm just the package you need to courier to Bakhara, remember?'

Slowly he shook his head, his eyes never leaving hers. He held her pinioned just with the force of that look. Her limbs felt heavy as if invisibly weighted.

How could he *do* that?

A flutter of apprehension stirred. No other man had the power to make her feel anything like it.

'You're far more than that and you know it, Soraya.'

Her brow puckered. There was something in his tone she couldn't fathom. A keen edge that matched the coil of tension swirling its way down to the pit of her stomach.

'I thought you were here to whisk me back to the hotel.' He said nothing. 'Why *are* you here, then?' After his threat back at the chateau, she'd put nothing past him.

'Hussein entrusted me with your safety. You're my responsibility till you return to Bakhara and—'

'I'm perfectly capable. I don't need to be watched over.' Indignation welled.

'Be that as it may, I was concerned when I found you gone. You're in unfamiliar territory, alone, when by your own admission you have limited experience of foreign travel. I needed to make sure you were all right.'

His voice rang with sincerity and abruptly Soraya's bubble of anger punctured. He was doing his job. It wasn't his fault it felt like he was her own personal gaoler. As for his disapproval— she saw no evidence of it now.

'Why did you come *here*?' He reached for his coffee.

'You make it sound as if Amboise is an unusual choice. It's a quaint old town with a chateau, cliff dwellings—'

'Not the town. *Here*.' His gesture encompassed both the old house and the sweep of park-like gardens she'd yet to explore. 'It's pleasant, but it doesn't match the opulence of the royal chateaux.'

'And, of course, I should be interested in opulence, is that it?' What did he think, that she'd somehow snaffled the Emir for his wealth?

Was that why Zahir had installed her in that beautiful, luxurious hotel that, to her overwrought nerves, felt ridiculously like a gilded prison?

'That's just it.' He leaned forward. 'I don't know what interests you.' His gaze dropped from her face. 'Apart from shoes with more sex appeal than substance.'

A flush rose from the vicinity of her ankles where the scarlet straps of her wedge-heeled espadrilles ended in saucy bows. Heat flooded up her thighs, through her body and scorched its way to her cheeks.

Because he thought her shoes sexy.

Her heart gave an odd little flutter.

Why did that observation sound like an admission of some sort? And why did it unsettle her so?

Zahir lifted his espresso but he didn't look away. Soraya gulped down some icy water, hoping to ease the rush of blood under her skin.

'Clos Lucé is where Leonardo da Vinci lived the final years of his life.'

'I thought he was Italian?'

'He was, but the King of France thought him so special he offered him a home.' She nodded to the open window above them. 'He slept in that room.'

'So you're a fan of his art?'

She shrugged. 'I never saw the Mona Lisa in Paris. There were too many other things to do.'

Zahir's eyebrows rose. 'Hussein mentioned you were studying art history in Paris.'

'I was.' Her chin tilted higher, on the defensive now.

Zahir said nothing but his silence told her he was waiting. For long moments she held his gaze, then she shrugged. What was the point in prevaricating?

'It wasn't my idea, it was my father's. He thought an understanding of art would be useful given my...future. A sort of wider cultural education.' What he hadn't said, of course, was that studying art was more genteel, more suitable for a lady. Not that he'd ever say that out loud.

Soraya smiled. Her dad had never quite understood her interest in the unfeminine sciences, but he was her staunchest ally against the traditionalists who'd looked down their noses at her chosen path. They'd seen her lack of interest in the usual female occupations as dangerous—a possible sign she was like her unnatural mother.

Her smile faded.

'Soraya?'

She looked up to find Zahir's eyes narrowing. 'Sorry?'

'You didn't enjoy the course?'

'No, I did. It's not what I would have chosen myself but it was interesting.' She paused, relishing the warmth of the filtered sunlight and the gentle bird calls, the sense, illusory as it was, of freedom.

'I should have made an effort to see his art. He was gifted in so many fields. Did you *see* the models of his inventions?' That had been such fun, especially when she'd met two amateur inventors eager to discuss them.

'I saw them.' His voice told her Leonardo's breakthroughs were mildly interesting to him, no more.

'Where do you think the world would be without people like that, finding new ways to solve problems?'

'What, like that multi-barrelled gun to mow down as many people as possible at a time?'

Soraya found herself smiling ruefully into eyes that had lost their hard edge and crinkled appealingly at the corners. That hint of amusement eased the hard lines of Zahir's face, making him more relaxed, not the stern figure of the last few days.

She'd thought him in his mid-thirties. Now she reassessed. He was younger than she'd assumed.

'It takes the gloss off his "man of the arts" image, doesn't it? But he was working on what people wanted.'

'You could say that about nuclear weapons.'

'True. It's the age-old issue, isn't it? What people do with what scientists invent.'

'That's what interests you? Science?' His eyes widened a fraction.

'Careful, Zahir. You're not in danger of typecasting me because I'm female, are you?' She'd come up against enough raised eyebrows in Bakhara for her supposedly unconventional interests. Inevitably she felt disappointment stir. 'Women aren't all interested in the same things. We're as varied as men.'

'So I'm learning.'

Soraya raised her eyebrows. Her guess was he expected women to focus on luxury and be dependent on men to make the decisions. No wonder they had been at loggerheads.

'If you weren't so interested in art history, why were you concerned to finish your project before you left?'

She sat back in her chair, surveying him carefully. 'You are sharp, aren't you?'

'I could say the same about you.' This time she caught it—a tiny flash of appreciation in his eyes. She felt an answering flicker of pleasure. 'Are you going to tell me what you were doing or is it a secret?'

'No secret. I just took more than one class.'

He said nothing, simply put down his cup and waited, as if he had all the time in the world and nothing more important to do than listen. Yet that stiff, judgemental attitude was missing. What had changed?

'Not really a class, actually. A job.'

'You *worked*?'

She couldn't help it. A gurgle of laughter escaped at his astonished expression. 'Is that so hard to believe?' She held up her hand. 'No, don't answer. I can guess—you thought I pretended to study but secretly majored in shopping.'

A twist of his lips told her she was on the right track. Despite her amusement, annoyance stirred.

'I'm rather fond of shopping, actually. Paris is a real treat for that—everything from haute couture to street markets.'

Soraya looked down at her shoes, but instead of remembering her thrill at getting such a bargain it was a different thrill entirely that rippled through her. Had she imagined the heat in Zahir's stare? He'd made her feel *sexy* with that casual reference to her footwear.

Her skin tingled and her blood throbbed with that weird, unfamiliar blast of heat. Unfamiliar till three days ago, that was. Till Zahir had singled her out in that bar.

She lifted her head.

'That night in the bar. Why did you stare at me like that?'

Zahir read the curiosity in her gaze and knew he'd seriously underestimated her. She had a sharp intellect as well as a strong streak of independence—characteristics he admired.

Yet he hadn't wanted to like her since the moment he'd seen her with another man. Had he let that blind him to other aspects of her character? Had he rushed to judgement?

'I was assessing the situation. You wouldn't have liked me interrupting your night out.'

Her head tilted to one side. Her brow wrinkled and her mouth pouted in a moue of concentration.

Zahir's breathing shallowed as he stared at those lush lips. He dragged his gaze to her dark eyes.

'No, that's not right.' She shook her head. 'You had no compunction about interrupting my night out. Once you decided to make your move, that was it.'

If he'd decided to 'make his move', that night would have ended very differently.

The thought exploded out of nowhere as he imagined doing what he'd been tempted to do on the dance floor—not release her, as she'd demanded, but sling her over his shoulder and carry her somewhere private where he could ravage her sultry mouth and possess her seductive body with the thorough attention they deserved.

A flash of incendiary heat roared through Zahir's veins, tightening his body to instant, painful readiness. His hand clenched so hard on the tiny coffee cup, he feared he'd break the handle. With stiff fingers he released it and slid his hand from the table.

With one casual remark she'd accelerated his pulse from zero to the speed of sound in an instant. It was unprecedented. It was *dangerous*.

'Zahir?' Dark eyes searched his. This time the throb of electricity between them was more than sexual. It struck right at his core, as if she could do the impossible and delve into his psyche. 'Why did you watch me like that?'

She was persistent. And naïve, he realised with shock, if she really had to ask. If she had any sense, she'd leave such questions safely unspoken. Was she more naïve than he'd assumed? The notion disturbed him.

Or was this a double bluff from a woman who knew her sexual power and was trying to toy with him?

Resentment surfaced. He was no woman's pawn.

'I assumed you wouldn't want me approaching the table and discussing your business in front of everyone.'

He saw from her frown she wasn't satisfied with his answer.

'But you sat there for *ages*.'

Silently he held her gaze. He had no intention of pandering to her ego by explaining a response that shouldn't be: his instant, logic-destroying attraction to Hussein's chosen bride.

Damn it. Why couldn't Hussein have sent someone else— a whole team of someone elses—to bring his fiancée home?

His heart plunged. The answer was easy. Because Zahir was the one Hussein trusted above all.

Shame drenched him.

Abruptly he shoved his chair back across the gravel and shot to his feet.

'Did you want to see the grounds?'

'You don't need to stay. I'll meet you back at the hotel.' From the corner of his eye he saw her spring to her feet. Eager for more sightseeing? Or for another chance to escape his vigilance?

For the first time in years Zahir felt unsure. Usually instinct

combined with thorough research gave him all the certainty
he needed. With Soraya he'd skipped the research, believing
this a quick, simple task. As for instinct... He firmed his lips
against a bitter laugh. He no longer trusted his instincts where
she was concerned.

'I have no other pressing business.' He slipped some cash
under his cup and gestured for her to lead the way, ignoring
the flash of dismay in her dark eyes. 'I'm curious to see what
the place has to offer.' Especially if it meant getting to know
the real Soraya Karim.

CHAPTER SIX

Soraya told herself she was disappointed he didn't give her the choice to explore alone. Yet disappointment didn't explain the curling awareness in the pit of her stomach, nor the tingle of heat between her shoulder blades where his gaze rested as she led the way down the path beside the wide sweep of lawn.

They stopped at a model of a spiral blade for a flying machine, big enough for a person to stand beneath and turn the handle to make it rotate.

'It's more elegant than the modern design.' She tried hard to focus on the model rather than the man beside her. Her nostrils twitched appreciatively at the scent of his warm skin with a hint of desert spice. She'd carried that scent on her own skin after wearing his jacket. It disturbed her how much she relished it.

'Personally I don't care how it looks,' he drawled. 'So long as it keeps me in the air. I'd rather a modern chopper that works than one that looks elegant.'

Soraya huffed with amusement and looked up at the sail turning above her head. She didn't want to relax with Zahir, for there was an undercurrent between them that unsettled her. These tiny hints of dry humour appealed to her too much. It was far easier not to like him.

'That's my line. I'm supposed to be the one focused on functionality.'

She smiled as a big family group arrived with children eager to experiment, then she led the way downhill to where more models of inventions studded the wooded grounds.

'Because you're a scientist?'

'Engineer. I qualified before I left Bakhara.' She flashed a look over her shoulder but no hint of surprise marred those indecently attractive features.

Swiftly she looked away, stopping before a model of a paddle-wheel boat and pretending to survey it closely.

The other group caught up with them again and children of all ages swarmed over the model, while some tiny tots crouched by the stream, playing a complicated game with sticks and leaves.

'That explains why you asked for directions to a power plant.' Zahir's words drew her attention.

'Sorry?'

'The concierge showed me the places you were interested in seeing.'

'Oh.' She'd forgotten to ask how he'd found her. Zahir must have searched for hours, yet instead of being angry he'd shown only curiosity. Every time she thought she had him pegged, he surprised her again.

'I visited a chateau instead. Far more *opulent* and appealing than a utilitarian power station.'

His chuckle surprised her, sneaking across her skin like a caress. A traitorous part of her enjoyed sharing a joke with him, wanted to see him smile at her.

Abruptly she turned and moved away down the path. She couldn't remember ever being so responsive to a man.

Or was it simply that she'd never spent time alone with such an attractive man? Had lack of exposure made her susceptible? She'd had no trouble keeping her head around her colleagues. But from the moment her gaze had locked with Zahir's she'd felt a zap of high-voltage connection. She couldn't shake it and that made her nervous.

'Somehow I suspect that's not why you changed your mind about visiting it.'

'It's not a state-of-the-art facility so I didn't bother.' Especially as nuclear power wasn't her field.

Not that she'd *have* a field once she became wife to the Emir.

'Is what you were doing in Paris? Engineering?'

'Yes. I was lucky enough to land work as assistant in a research project. Mainly I was just calculating data.'

'You must be good to be taken on.'

His simple statement warmed her. In the Women's University in Bakhara there'd been few interested in engineering. Most people viewed her choice as a misguided attempt to prove herself in a male domain. Or proof that she was unfeminine. Many in Bakhara clung to tradition.

'My professor recommended me. She thought even if I was in Paris for the cultural experience it would be a crime not to take advantage of the opportunity.'

'She was right. Opportunities are there to be grabbed. Did you enjoy the work?'

'Loved it! The team was excellent and I learned so much. I—' She looked down at her hands, clenched too tight before her.

'You…?'

She shook her head. What was the point of saying she'd planned to take part in the project's next phase—that the team leader had asked her to take on more responsibility? That she'd begun to see a future for herself that had nothing to do with a royal marriage and everything to do with her own interests and professional skills?

Ruthlessly she cut off the regrets that churned under the surface. No point going there.

'Look at this.' She quickened her pace to circle a large wooden shell. 'An early model for a war tank. Who'd have thought it?'

Zahir watched her duck her head and step up into the structure. A flash of shapely legs drew his eye but he managed not to stare. Her dress was light and summery rather than revealing, but the way she filled it in all the right places would be pure distraction to any red-blooded man.

Soraya was a captivating mix. She made a show of keeping him at arm's length but regularly forgot and relaxed into unguarded moments. She was intelligent and sexy, a woman he enjoyed crossing swords with.

Until he remembered pleasure was an emotion he shouldn't feel around Hussein's fiancée.

Yet that didn't prevent him wondering what she'd been going to say. She didn't hide her emotions as well as she imagined and he had no doubt she'd changed the subject rather than pursue a line of thought that bothered her. Something about the team she worked with in Paris.

'Your friends at the club the other night—are they engineers too?'

'Sorry?' She looked up, her eyes wide as if surprised at the change of subject.

'The guy you danced with. Does he work on the same project?'

Was it imagination or did her lips tighten?

'No. They're from the university but not in my field.'

Zahir waited for her to elaborate but she said nothing.

'So you don't have a passion for engineering in common?'

'Who? Me and Raoul? Hardly.' She stepped down, pretending not to notice the arm he extended to steady her.

'What do you have in common? You seemed *very* close.'

Her head jerked up and her eyes clashed with his. Sparks of sensation flared and burst across his skin like a brush fire igniting from a summer-lightning strike. It disturbed him that he'd never known such a reaction to a woman. Even in the throes of first and only love, it had taken more than a look to set his blood simmering.

'That's none of your business.' Soraya's breathing shallowed. Zahir became tantalisingly aware of her breasts' jagged rise and fall as she struggled to remain calm.

'It is, when I'm taking you home to marry Hussein.' He let

the words crash out, harsh and honest, as if saying them would break the strange spell she wove around him.

Something had to.

Her eyes rounded and her mouth formed an 'O' of shock. Finally she found her voice.

'Is that what you were doing all that time? Spying on me?' Her voice rose in outrage.

Zahir said nothing. He'd had no plan that night other than to track her down and tell her about Hussein's request that she return. It had been the shock of seeing her. The shock of recognition that had rooted him to the spot. As if he *knew* her, not as the subject of his next mission, but as someone intrinsically important to *himself.*

For once he hadn't known how to proceed. Not when his overwhelming impulse had been to ignore his mission and stake a personal claim on her.

Guilt pooled in his belly. No wonder he'd made a hash of everything that night.

'I don't spy,' Zahir said at last. 'But I won't shy from telling Hussein anything I feel he should know.'

'Like the fact that I had the temerity to *dance* with a man in a public place?' She shook her head. 'What century did you crawl out of, Zahir?'

'If it was only dances, I'm sure Hussein won't be concerned.' He paused, telling himself his urgent need to know was pure altruism. A favour to a friend. 'Is that all there was, Soraya?'

Colour seeped across her cheekbones and her eyes snapped a warning. 'My personal life is just that. Personal. If the Emir has questions, he can ask me himself.'

Her chin jutted belligerently as she faced him toe-to-toe. He applauded her backbone. Few men in Bakhara or elsewhere would have stood up to him this way.

'What about your friend's invitation when you got home?' The words slipped out before he could reconsider. 'She asked you to join her and her lover in bed. Does your bridegroom have a right to know if you make a habit of sharing so *intimately* with your flatmate?'

Her head jerked back, her cheeks leaching of colour as she goggled up at him.

He opened his mouth to speak again—to say what, he didn't know—when her laughter erupted. It had a ragged, raw quality that spoke of disbelief, amusement and something else that made him wish he'd kept his mouth shut.

'You heard that?' She shook her head, wiping her eyes. 'Then it's a shame you didn't hear Lisle mention her twin sister was visiting and they were in her room having a catch-up since her boyfriend had left.' Her hand dropped and her eyes sizzled defiantly.

'Don't presume to judge me by the standards of others. Or are they your standards, Zahir?' She raised a hand when he'd have spoken. 'No, don't tell me. Contrary to your lurid imaginings, I didn't lead a life of debauchery in Paris, nor did I develop a taste for threesomes.'

It was the truth. He read it in every outraged bone in her stiffly held body. In the shock shadowing her eyes and the distaste twisting her full lips.

More than that, he felt it deep within, a truth he'd deliberately ignored.

Why? Why draw conclusions on such flimsy evidence when he'd spent a lifetime learning balanced judgement?

Because he'd needed a reason not to like her.

Because from the instant he'd clapped eyes on her he'd felt an attraction so strong he'd sought any excuse to pretend it didn't exist. It had rocked his world, as if the earth's tectonic plates had shifted beneath his feet.

Because distrusting her gave him a reason not to acknowledge that inexplicable attraction. He'd hidden behind it rather than face the truth.

'Do you always leap to conclusions about people?'

'No.' He shook his head. 'Never.'

'Just with me?' Her sceptical look froze as she read his face.

'Yes.' Shame burned him. Soraya was right. He'd taken one look at her and his judgement, his brain, had shut down. 'I'm sorry, Soraya.' He held her gaze, restraining himself against the impulse to step forward and comfort her. As if she'd welcome his touch! 'That was crass of me, as well as wrong. I apologise unreservedly. The accusation was unworthy of you.'

'So now you pretend to know me? That's rich.'

'I don't know you. That's why I'm here now, because I want to understand you.'

'To spy for the Emir.'

'No!' What a mess he'd made of this. No one would ever believe him the same man who brokered multinational deals on a regular basis.

'Then why?' The anger had gone from her eyes, replaced by a searching curiosity as strong as his own.

Zahir drew in a fortifying breath. He owed her the truth, no matter how vulnerable it made him.

'For myself. Because I need to.'

Her eyes widened and his heart crashed faster as he read comprehension in her eyes. Soraya stared so hard she didn't even seem to notice the straggling group of families pass by— adults, a couple of teenagers and younger children.

'No,' she said at last. 'I don't want you here.'

'Soraya, I'm truly sorry. I—'

'It's not because of what you…assumed about me. I'd just rather be alone.' Zahir's stomach knotted as he read awareness in her dark gaze and a flicker of fear.

He should be relieved one of them was behaving wisely.

She turned away. 'I'll see you back at the hotel.'

Zahir knew it was the right thing to do. Some things were better hidden and never acknowledged. Yet not following her took far more will-power than it should.

He stood, watching her go, until a curve in the path brought the family group back in view. He saw two empty prams and one of the toddlers holding the hand of an older child.

Frowning, he surveyed the group, checking his recollection from when their paths had crossed before.

His heart kicked up a pace as adrenalin surged. He wasn't mistaken: the group wasn't complete. It was the sort of detail he'd been trained to notice. He breathed deep, double-checking.

The toddler in the yellow T-shirt was missing.

Even as the thought formed in his head, Zahir loped onto the track, cutting across Soraya's path.

'Zahir, I'd really rather—'

He quickened his pace, away from the families and back in the direction they'd come. The area was lightly forested and open enough to see for some way. Unless the child was down near the tempting little rivulets that meandered through the grounds.

Zahir's neck prickled as he jogged forward.

'Zahir?' She must have followed him.

Then he saw it: a flare of sunshine-yellow in the shadows. *In the glinting water.* His heart seemed to judder to a stop mid-beat even as he broke into a run.

'Here,' he called over his shoulder. 'Ambulance!' He didn't pause to see if she caught the phone he tossed.

'Soraya? Are you okay?'

She looked up, tugged from her thoughts by Zahir's rich baritone. Around them the discreet chatter of the hotel restaurant resurfaced, the sense of being with others, even if in a secluded corner of the great gilded dining salon. The sky glowed with the sun's last syrupy, pink light as indigo darkness closed in from the forest, cutting off the chateau from the outside world.

It was peaceful and pleasant. So different from the scene branded on her brain. The toddler's face, that awful waxen colour. The screams of his mother. The dreadful, wrenching terror that had reduced everything to slow motion.

Even now the remembered scent of fear clogged her nostrils, vying with the rich scents of their superb meal.

'I'm fine. Thank you.' She cast Zahir a perfunctory smile and lifted a morsel of fish to her mouth. Yet her limbs still felt ridiculously shaky. As if she'd run for her life that day, not simply called the medics and corralled the toddler's family while Zahir had saved his life.

She hadn't even realised there *was* an emergency. She'd been so absorbed, thinking about Zahir, how he'd insulted her then apologised so gravely she'd had no choice but to believe he regretted it. Especially when his eyes mirrored her own deep confusion. She'd struggled to grasp what had happened even as Zahir hauled the boy from the creek and puffed air into his little lungs.

Her knife and fork clattered onto her plate.

'Thank heaven you were there today. If you hadn't been, if you hadn't noticed he was missing—'

'There's no point dwelling on "what ifs". The child is safe.' Zahir reached across the table as if to take her hand where it clenched in a tense fist on the linen cloth. At the last moment he reached instead for his water.

Soraya knew she should be glad he didn't invade her personal space. Yet that didn't douse her longing for the comfort of his touch. Despite the long soak in her suite's oversized bath, she still felt chilled by the afternoon's events. Zahir's hand would be warm, solid and real.

'I know,' she murmured. 'I can't help it. I keep going over it again and again in my head.' She drew a shuddery breath and reached for her glass.

'It was a shock. That's a natural reaction.' There was understanding in his voice.

'*You* weren't shocked.' She bit her lip. 'I'm sorry. I didn't mean for that to sound like an accusation.'

'I understand.' The ghost of a smile softened his mouth and that invisible thread of connection between them twanged tighter, dragging at her internal muscles. 'Don't worry, I was running on adrenalin too. It's just that I've been in emergency situations before. Too often.'

That glimmer of a smile died, obliterated by a sudden harshness that transformed his features. It reminded her that she knew next to nothing about this man with whom she would spend the next few weeks—more, since he was the Emir's right-hand man. In Bakhara their paths would cross regularly.

'Tell me. Please.' Her words escaped without conscious thought and she met his surprised gaze. 'It's none of my business I know. I just...' Soraya bit her lip, not understanding her compulsion to know him. It had nothing to do with prurient curiosity and everything to do with the awareness that had shimmered so strongly between them this afternoon. From the first it had been there. He'd all but acknowledged it himself today.

She needed to know what it was.

'I don't *understand* you.' The words tumbled from her lips. 'And this afternoon...'

How did she explain something fundamental had shifted today when they'd shared laughter and she'd glimpsed a man who appealed far too much, when he'd apologised so sincerely she'd felt his shame and then when he'd saved that child? He wasn't the cold, arrogant man she'd tried to cast him. He was so much more.

She sensed it was dangerous to like Zahir too much. She'd felt safe in her indignation. Yet she couldn't keep pretending he was her unfeeling enemy. It just didn't ring true.

'If it had been left to his family he'd have drowned. They wouldn't have realised till too late.' The words burst out. 'If I'd been there without you, as I said I wanted, I wouldn't have been able to save him either. Only *you*—'

'Don't beat yourself up, Soraya.' His voice was calm, mellow and reassuring. 'You did wonderfully, keeping everyone in order till the medics came.'

Strong fingers covered hers and instantly heat seeped back along her veins.

She'd been right. There was magic in Zahir's touch. This time she wasn't going to question it or pull away.

A sense of wellbeing grew, a glow that wasn't simply the

physical warmth of flesh touching flesh. She looked from their joined hands then up into eyes that had darkened to the colour of the encircling forest.

'I want to understand.' Though she wasn't sure what exactly she needed to know. It was all tangled together—today's events and the enigma of Zahir's true personality. This...*something* between them. The unsettling realisation she didn't understand herself as well as she'd thought.

Absently he rubbed his thumb over her hand and some of the tightness in her belly unravelled. Her rigid shoulders dropped a fraction.

'There's not much to understand. I've seen violence in my life, too often. I learned to react quickly. Even as a child.'

'So young?' At her query his mouth twisted and he looked down at their joined hands.

'One of my first memories is of blood pooling across a stone floor and wondering why the man with the funny stare didn't move before the red stained his clothes.'

'Oh, Zahir.' Her free hand closed over his as he held her. 'I'm so sorry.'

He shrugged. 'It was no one I knew. Just one of my father's cronies.' He spoke with such matter-of-fact coolness it sent a tiny quiver through her. 'He'd had too much to drink and was unsteady on his feet. When he fell, he cracked his skull.'

'How old were you?'

'Three, perhaps. Maybe four.'

'That's dreadful.' Something deep inside twisted. He'd been so young. So vulnerable. What had his life been like that he'd come across such a scene?

'I remember my father stumbling across the room, cursing about the mess. And making myself scarce. I was good at that.' His mouth was a flat line, no trace of insouciance now.

Soraya felt him stiffen under her touch and wondered what he was remembering. The look on his face as much as his words told her it hadn't been pleasant. What had his mother been doing while her son had watched that horrible scene?

'There were other…incidents too. Enough to learn how swift and unpredictable violence can be.' His gaze fixed on a point beyond her but she wondered if what he saw was far beyond the walls of the hotel. 'It was useful training, in a way. It meant I was always half-prepared.'

Soraya blinked and stared. Zahir painted a picture that, despite the lack of detail, horrified her. A childhood where the most valuable lesson learned was a readiness to confront violence.

'It sounds like your childhood was eventful.'

Swiftly he turned his gaze on her and she caught a flicker of amusement in his eyes. 'Obviously Hussein knows what he's doing, choosing you as his wife. That's a diplomatic response if ever I heard one.'

He looked down and frowned as if registering for the first time their linked hands. Abruptly he drew his away, leaving her oddly bereft.

She laced her fingers together and slipped her hands into her lap. They still held the imprint of his, hard and comforting against hers.

'My early childhood was a disaster, but I survived. Then I joined the royal household. I was safe, well-fed, educated, comfortable. But I trained with the warriors. I saw my share of accidents and wounds. I could diagnose a dislocation, a broken bone or sprain by the age of twelve.'

'That must have been tough.'

'I loved it.' Zahir's sudden grin took her by surprise and she sat back, her pulse thudding an uneven response to the sheer glory of it.

Oh my. Oh. My!

It was the second time she'd glimpsed the man behind the wall of steel. The first, when he'd threatened her with such fervour if she ever injured the Emir. And now a look of such unadulterated joy it was like swallowing sunshine, just seeing it. It took Soraya a moment to find her voice.

'Why did you love it?'

He picked up his cutlery but didn't move to eat. 'I belonged,' he said at last. 'That became my world.'

Soraya frowned, more curious than ever for details. But she had no right to push for what was clearly private and difficult territory. As it was, she sensed Zahir had revealed more than he usually deigned to share.

'Eventually I joined the Emir's bodyguard, even led it. So you see I've had lots of opportunities to deal with crises.' His smile now was more restrained, a polite curve of the lips only, not that blinding flash of pleasure that had thwacked her senses into overdrive.

'But no one would want to harm the Emir.' She, more than most of his subjects, had cause to know what a generous and honourable man he was.

Zahir shook his head. 'There is always the possibility—from someone who seeks fame through a violent act, to someone disturbed or ruthless. There have been times when noticing a small detail, or sensing something amiss, made all the difference.'

Soraya slid her hands up to rub her arms. 'Like noticing that boy wasn't with his family.'

Zahir nodded. 'I was trained to register the smallest details. To take note and act quickly when necessary.'

'No one asked you to monitor them.'

His straight shoulders lifted. 'You don't entirely switch off even when you're no longer on close personal protection duty. I haven't done that for years but the skills stay with you.'

'Just as well.'

He shot her a quick glance but she felt its intensity to the tips of her toes.

'Eat, Soraya. It's over. The child is safe and the family reunited. There's nothing to worry about.'

She picked up her cutlery and made a show of eating her meal, as he did. But her niggle of anxiety grew rather than faded with the knowledge she'd gained.

It had all been easier when she could write Zahir off as bossy, arrogant and interfering. Before he'd revealed a humanity and tenderness that made a mockery of her easy assumptions. He'd thought badly of her, but his apology had been genuine and his contrition real. She'd seen the shame and regret in his eyes. And at least he'd been up-front with her.

She recalled him, his clothes plastered to his tall body, cradling the toddler and crooning to him once he had begun to breathe again. He hadn't turned a hair when the child vomited comprehensively and begun to cry. He'd been patience itself with both the boy and his distraught mother, managing to calm them both and monitoring them till professional help had arrived.

The sight of the small child held so easily and safely against Zahir's powerful frame ignited a blast of emotions Soraya couldn't label, but felt to her core.

Nor had he been eager for acknowledgement. As soon as the child was with medical staff he'd taken Soraya's trembling hand, offered his best wishes to the group and led her away for a restorative coffee. He hadn't turned a hair at the stares he'd received with his muddied trousers and his wet shirt clinging to his powerful torso. He'd been solicitous of *her*, as if she'd been the one injured.

Zahir was quietly competent, caring, strong when she was weak.

And he…appealed to her.

He appealed too much for a woman who wasn't interested in men. Who'd seen the pitfalls of romance and decided early not to go there. That had been one of the reasons she'd agreed to her royal betrothal—the belief that an arranged marriage to an honourable man was safer than a so-called love match.

She'd never been romantically interested in any man. Given her background, maybe she'd even worked a little too hard to avoid such temptation.

Why then did Zahir fascinate her so? Why did she need to understand him?

Because she wasn't as self-sufficient as she'd thought?

Because, perhaps, she was susceptible to the charm of a strong, handsome man? A man who hid surprising gentleness and a mile-wide streak of heroism behind a cool façade?

CHAPTER SEVEN

TWO DAYS later Soraya and Zahir returned to the hotel to find a familiar family group in the car park.

'Mademoiselle Karim!' a teenage girl called out. Soraya remembered her; she'd been pale and distraught, blaming herself for her little brother's accident.

'Lucie, how are you? How is your brother?' Soraya smiled as she neared the group, pleasure filling her as she saw the little boy safe in his mother's arms.

'Recovered fully, as you see.' The older woman smiled tentatively before glancing at her husband, clearly uncomfortable beside her. 'We came to thank you both.' Her gaze rested on Zahir. 'Without you…'

'Without them he would have died,' her husband said, his voice harsh. 'Because you couldn't watch him.'

Soraya stiffened, stunned at the venom in his tone.

'In my experience,' said a firm baritone beside her, 'a man casts blame when he holds himself responsible but hasn't the guts to acknowledge it.' Zahir stood so close she felt the fury emanating from him. 'It's a father's duty to protect his family.'

The bristling man before them seemed to deflate. Enough to reveal the hollowed eyes and pallor of a man still working through shock.

'It's very hot out here,' Soraya said quickly. 'Why don't we go inside for a cool drink?' She smiled at the children. 'Or ice-cream? They have terrific ice-cream here.'

* * *

It was a relief to escape outside again with the children. Despite Soraya's calming presence and his own tight control, Zahir could barely stomach being with a man who refused to accept responsibility for his son's safety and blamed his womenfolk for his shortcomings.

'Well done!' Zahir congratulated one of the girls on her archery skills. 'You hit the target this time. Now, try it again, but don't forget to hold the bow this way.' He leaned in to demonstrate.

He glanced at the window where Soraya sat with their older guests, her smile warm. The mother had relaxed enough to relinquish the toddler into Soraya's arms and she bounced him on her knees. Even the woman's husband had unwound enough to nod at something she said.

Zahir's dislike for the man would have stifled the atmosphere. The child's father had struck his personal sore spot: neglectful fathers topped his list of dislikes.

He shook his head as he helped one of the children aim her bow.

Soraya had marshalled the group before he'd even got a grip on his anger. She'd charmed them all, reassured them and acted as hostess as if born to it. He remembered how she'd organised the crowd at the accident. Without her it would have been mayhem.

Her skills would make her perfect in the role of Hussein's queen. She was gracious, charming and able to put people at ease in difficult circumstances.

Hussein had chosen his bride well. Socially accomplished, quick thinking and feisty enough to hint at a passionate nature. She would make a fine wife: an asset in public and the sort of spouse a man rejoiced to come home to at the end of a long day.

The realisation should have reassured him that his mission to return her to Bakhara was important. But it brought no pleasure.

Just a twist in his gut that felt horribly like envy.

* * *

'You've got an ice-cream addiction, Soraya.'

'*I* have?' She looked at the remains of the double-scoop pistachio-and-coffee ice-cream he held and shook her head. 'I don't hear you complaining.'

Zahir shrugged and she averted her eyes lest they cling too long to the movement of his broad shoulders. She'd discovered a weakness for Zahir's wide, straight shoulders and rare, spectacular smile.

She looked instead around the stone-built town. Its square was hung with flags for Bastille Day and lights in the plane trees had just been turned on. In the background a small but enthusiastic band entertained onlookers.

'I'm just keeping you company.' Zahir's deep voice tickled her senses. 'Being a good companion.'

As he had been ever since Amboise. It was as if his accusation and apology, not to mention the crisis there, had cleared the air between them. No word of reproach or disapproval passed his lips. Nor—and she told herself she was relieved by it—did he refer to the shimmering attraction between them.

She'd begun to wonder if, after all, it was one-sided. Who wouldn't be star-struck by a man like Zahir? Even if his attention was for her as bride to his mentor.

'Watch out!' She saw the football before Zahir yet he managed to whip around and stop its wayward trajectory. He kicked it up, bouncing it easily off his knees and feet as he scanned the playing field beside the river.

A grinning boy waved and Zahir kicked the ball straight to him.

'You play football?'

'I used to. When I was young.'

'Me too.'

'Why aren't I surprised?' A slow grin spread across his face and Soraya wondered if she'd ever be able to see it without her pulse stuttering out of control.

'What else did you do when you were young?' They'd been

careful to avoid personal topics. They discussed France and the places they saw, or politics and books.

The one subject they never touched on was Bakhara.

'I rode. I discovered chess. I learned to fight.'

Soraya laughed. 'Of course. You sound like a traditional Bakhari male.'

'I *am* a traditional Bakhari male.'

She shook her head. A traditionalist wouldn't have let her drive his precious car, or listen attentively to a woman explaining the principles of geothermal power.

'What did you do when you were young?'

'Learn to cook, keep house and embroider.' She sighed, remembering hours of dutiful boredom. 'And sneaked out to play football.'

'And dreamed of marrying a handsome prince?'

'No!' The word shot out sharply. 'Never that.'

Zahir watched her intently. 'Marrying Hussein isn't the fulfilment of a lifelong ambition? I thought little girls fixated on a glamorous marriage.'

Soraya lifted her ice-cream, hoping the cherry flavour would counteract the sour tang on her tongue. 'Other little girls maybe. Marriage was never my dream.'

'But things are different now.'

'Oh yes, they're different now.' Bitterness welled, and with it anger at the limitations placed on her life by her engagement. 'Can we not talk about it now? I'd rather concentrate on this.' She waved a hand to encompass the crowd and the holiday atmosphere.

'Besides—' she nodded in the direction of the playing field '—I think you're wanted.'

The football sailed through the air to land near Zahir. The same grinning teenager waved for him to join the impromptu game.

Zahir shook his head. 'I can't leave you.'

'Of course you can. I'm perfectly fine.' She reached to pull his jacket off one shoulder then stopped as a sizzle of fire shot through her fingertips. Beneath her touch his muscles stiffened. His eyes darkened and her breath snagged as heat pulsed between them.

Just one touch did that.

'Go,' she said hoarsely, her hand dropping. 'Please.' She needed time alone to regroup. So much for her innocent belief that things were easier between them. On the surface their relationship was pleasant, friendly, even. But beneath the surface lurked emotions she didn't want to stir.

'If you wish.' He stripped his jacket off and handed it to her. 'Unless you'd prefer to play?'

That made her smile. 'It's you they want. Go.' Studiously she ignored the warmth of his jacket over her arm. She made a production of waving him off then leaned against a tree, watching him lope down to the field.

It didn't surprise her that he sided with the younger players who seemed outclassed by their more experienced rivals. Soraya had seen him with children before. He was a natural, treating them as equals, yet with a patience that made him a good teacher and role model.

She watched him sprint across the field, take the ball almost to the goal and deftly avoid several tackles till a boy of thirteen or so had time to join him. Zahir passed him the ball, then applauded as the boy's shot at goal missed by a whisker.

Pride surfaced. She *liked* Zahir, admired him. She wondered what he'd be like with his own children. She guessed he'd be fiercely loyal and supportive, a true friend. He'd be the same with the woman he loved.

Soraya caught the direction of her thoughts and slammed them shut with a gasp of horror.

Fixing her gaze on the river glinting beyond the playing field, she focused on the last few licks of her ice-cream and the sound of music filling the dusk.

A tentative voice intruded. 'Would you care to dance?' The man's smile was open and the hand he extended marked by hard work. She guessed he was a farmer with his craggy, sun-bronzed face. The music beckoned.

Why not? She'd promised herself she'd make the most of these last precious days of freedom. Placing Zahir's jacket and her bag of purchases on a nearby seat, Soraya took the stranger's hand.

Zahir felt like a kid again, light-hearted and spontaneous. He was even showing off for the girl in the floaty, floral dress standing in the shade at the edge of the square, as if he had nothing more on his mind than making the most of the day.

He couldn't remember the last time he'd felt this way. As if life was simple and full of pleasure, rather than a compli-cated series of manoeuvres to be plotted carefully, a contest to be won. More and more he felt it, the infectious joy of being with Soraya. As if weighty matters of state weren't the be-all and end-all of his existence. As if, imperceptibly, his priori-ties had changed.

The sensation was alluring. Like Soraya.

He glanced up, expecting to see her there, watching, but she'd gone. She was fine, he told himself. She'd be in the square, tasting local delicacies or chatting with someone. But a few minutes later he excused himself and jogged over to where he'd left her.

His jacket lay folded on a chair beside her cloth bag that was filled to the brim with her haul of goodies from the market stalls. He turned and surveyed the crowd. Sure enough, there she was, smiling as she danced with a husky young man. Her joy was infectious, even from this distance, and he wished it was him holding her as they danced over the cobblestones.

But discretion was the better part of valour. Holding Soraya would be inviting trouble. Instead he folded his arms and watched as the sky darkened and the woman who filled his thoughts moved from partner to partner.

* * *

'Time to stop?' Zahir's words interrupted her partner's thanks as the music ended. Soraya swung round, breathing heavily after that last mad polka. In the dim light Zahir loomed. Was that disapproval in his voice? His face was set in harsh lines she hadn't seen in days.

Instantly resentment stirred. And disappointment. She'd thought they were past the disapproval.

'Why?' She tucked a strand of hair behind her ear then crossed her arms defensively. 'Because I'm too boisterous? Because it's not the behaviour of a soon-to-be-queen?' His gaze bored into hers and, despite her annoyance, secret heat flared. The heat a woman felt for a man. 'Surely you don't think I'm flirting?'

'Nothing like that. You've been dancing nonstop and I thought you needed a rest.' His eyes skimmed the rapid rise of her breasts before he looked away.

'Sorry.' She ducked her head. 'I thought you were taking me to task.'

'Not surprising, given the way I jumped down your throat initially.'

Surprised, Soraya looked up. One thing about Zahir, he didn't hide from the facts. Even reminders of his mistakes. He wasn't like anyone else she knew. Or maybe it was her feelings for him that were unique.

'Dance with me?' The moment she said it she realised how much she wanted to.

'Surely you've had enough. Let me buy you a cold drink while we wait for the fireworks.'

Soraya shook her head. She wanted Zahir to hold her. She'd spent a lifetime doing the right thing, was facing a future of duty, and for this day wanted something for herself.

'Please, Zahir? Just one dance? It's Bastille Day, after all.' She held out her arms and after a long moment he took her in his arms, holding her gently and not too close. Even so her senses clamoured in delight as the music struck up and they moved together.

'You're not French. Bastille Day means nothing to you.'

'You're wrong.' She fought to keep her voice even when her bloodstream bubbled with pleasure. 'It's about liberty. There's nothing more important than freedom.'

Zahir heard the edge in her voice and tried to read her face in the darkness. She was like fluid quicksilver in his arms. He had to make an effort not to drag her close. Instead he focused on her words.

'Liberty? You speak as if it's threatened.'

She didn't answer for a moment. 'This is *my* time,' she said eventually. 'When I reach Bakhara I won't be able to do as I want or make my own choices. I'll be constrained.'

Because she'd be Hussein's bride.

'You don't sound enthusiastic.'

This time her silence was even longer. 'It's a great honour to be chosen as the Emir's bride.'

Yet he heard no pleasure in her voice. Or was it that he didn't want to hear it? Damn him for his jealousy.

'You're right,' he said at last. 'Your life will be restricted.' Hadn't his own become tightly constrained by duty, loyalty and the demands placed on it? Maybe that explained his dizzying sense of freedom with Soraya. This was a vacation from a life of responsibilities. Yet he couldn't help suspecting the wonder of it would continue if he had Soraya by his side, always. 'But there will be benefits. Hussein is a good man. He'll look after you.'

Though he shied from the thought of them together.

The music ended and they stopped moving in the shadows at the edge of the square. He told himself to let her go but didn't move. Nor did she.

'I know he is,' she said quietly. 'But it's an enormous step, giving up the life I know.'

Zahir breathed deep, dizzy with her sweet, fresh scent, revelling in the feel of her in his arms.

'Would you ever consider not going through with it?'

His hoarse words seemed over-loud in the charged silence.

Appalled, he wished he could retract them. What sort of mad, wishful thinking was that?

'Why would I do that?'

He told himself this was just a hypothetical discussion. 'If you fell for someone else.' Yet he held his breath as he waited for her answer, his pulse drumming in his ears.

'Imagine the fallout.' Her head drooped towards his chest so that he looked down on her vulnerable nape. He gathered her in to him. Just to comfort her, he assured himself. Yet his arms moulded to her as if they belonged.

She sighed. 'The scandal would be enormous, especially after my mother.'

'Your mother?'

'She disgraced herself and the family and my dad bore the brunt of disapproval for not vilifying her. Poor Dad, I couldn't do that to him. His business would be ruined and he'd be an outcast.'

And so would she, Zahir reminded himself. A man who truly cared for her wouldn't do that to her.

'Anyway, I'm pretty sure it's against the law to break a contract with the nation's ruler.' Her laugh was hollow. 'Besides.' She lifted her head and looked him straight in the eye. 'What man would dare steal the Emir's bride? He'd be punished, surely?'

Soraya's upturned face was beautiful, her eyes almost beseeching, and Zahir knew a crazy urge to kiss her till the world faded and all that was left was them.

'He'd lose all claim to honour or loyalty to the crown,' Zahir said slowly, feeling the full weight of such a prospect. He'd made honour and loyalty his life. 'He'd never be able to hold his head up again. He'd be stripped of official titles and positions and the council of elders would banish him from Bakhara.' He drew a deep breath. 'Hussein could never call him friend again.'

'As I thought.' Her hands dropped and she stepped abruptly out of his hold. 'No man would even consider it.'

CHAPTER EIGHT

It WASN'T *working*.

Zahir hefted in a determined breath and thrust off from the end of the pool, forcing his burning lungs and overworked body into another lap.

No matter how hard he pushed himself, he couldn't strip her from his mind. Soraya was there constantly.

He was at the end of his tether. Sleep grew elusive. His attempts to focus on the future and the governorship which would be his greatest challenge to date faded into the background. Soraya took centre stage.

He'd thought to change her mind about taking a slow route back to Bakhara since their time together was fraught with perilous undercurrents.

She'd said she wanted to see the countryside and he'd given it to her. They stayed in a friend's manor house in the Perigord, surrounded by walnut groves, tiny villages and winding narrow roads. No boutiques. No nightclubs.

Soraya loved it.

So much for his plans to convince her to cut short their stay and head for the bright lights! She found everything fascinating; from the stone-building styles to the local accent and the people they met. Even the limestone caves with their prehistoric paintings captured her interest.

Her delight in it all, her vivid joy in each moment, made

every experience fresh and new to him too. He was rediscovering simple pleasures.

Yet there was nothing simple or innocent about his feelings for her.

Zahir hauled himself from the water. It was still early and he was taking the chopper to Paris. Ostensibly it was a meeting that called him. In reality, it was as an excuse to absent himself from Soraya.

He enjoyed being with her too much. He found himself opening up to her. He'd even told her about his childhood, something he never shared. More than that, he felt emotions stirring that he had no business feeling. For years he'd locked emotions behind a wall of steel. Now it seemed there were fissures in the barricade he'd built around himself. He was a different man from the one who'd met her in Paris. He *felt* more, experienced more, cared more.

Zahir was halfway to the house when he saw the garage door open. He frowned. The old estate manager wouldn't be up at dawn working, but with the owners in Paris, who else could it be?

One step into the building and he knew.

The breath sucked from his lungs as he saw her on her back beneath an old four-wheel drive; neat sneakers, white socks and the most mouth-watering legs he'd ever seen.

With those light summer dresses she wore he'd had ample opportunity to recognise Soraya had world-class legs. But her clothes were always modest. Now for the first time his gaze trawled up past her knees to smooth, slim thighs that made him think of cool sheets and a hot woman, of passion and endless hours of erotic pleasure.

Humming off-key, Soraya wasn't sure at first, but she thought she heard swearing, low-voiced and urgent. She paused and wiped her brow with a grimy hand.

A stream of whispered words vied with the early-morning birdsong.

Her skin prickled as she realised she wasn't alone. An instant later she scooted out from beneath the vehicle.

Long legs were braced wide before her. Bare, sinewy feet. Powerfully muscled thighs in sodden board shorts. A towel clutched in one large, white-knuckled hand.

Soraya's throat dried as she yanked her gaze higher, skimming over a washboard abdomen, wide pectoral muscles and straight shoulders. Higher, till she got lost in green eyes turned dark and smoky in the early-morning light.

Her heart jumped and she sat up quickly.

'Zahir.' Her voice was breathless and high. She swallowed and tried again, ignoring the feverish pleasure that surged at the sound of his name on her lips. Ever since the Bastille Day celebrations she'd been ultra-aware of him.

Who was she kidding? She'd been aware of him from the start, only in the beginning she'd been able to hide behind dislike.

'You surprised me.' Great. Now her conversation had dried up with her brain.

Despite the affinity she felt for Zahir and her pleasure in his company, she grew more on edge daily.

It was as if another woman inhabited her body. A woman with desires and needs utterly foreign to her. A woman whose eyes followed this man's every move. Whose breasts were swollen and tender with longing for his touch. Who felt hunger curl hard in her belly just at the sound of his deep voice.

Maybe the critics of her childhood were right. Maybe after all she was doomed to follow in her mother's footsteps—unable to resist the lure of a handsome man. Perhaps her father's protectiveness had been well-founded, and her own innate caution, her wariness of intimacy, had been more valid than she'd realised.

At twenty-four she'd begun to think herself completely immune to the male sex, for none had ever stirred her blood.

Now she knew better.

Whatever it was she felt for Zahir, it wasn't immunity. It was wild and strong, exciting and frightening. Worse, it wasn't just because of his looks. She enjoyed his dry humour, his intelligence, the fact that he was a decent man who took his responsibilities seriously. He was marvellous with kids and patient with a woman spooked by her looming future.

'What are you wearing?' His voice was husky.

She glanced down, then hurriedly folded her legs close, wrapping her arms around them.

'I didn't have any shorts so I cut off some jeans. It's too hot for them here.'

She'd made a mess of the job. Sewing had never been her forte, to the dismay of her female relatives who'd spent so many hours trying to interest her in embroidery and a dozen other housewifely skills. She couldn't even hack the legs off her old jeans in a straight line!

Zahir's dark eyebrows crunched together. 'That doesn't explain why you're down in the dirt.'

Ridiculously his words reminded her of the scolds she'd received from aunts about unladylike behaviour. For a moment the old guilt rose: about the fact she was her mother's daughter. That she was impulsive and strong-willed. That she didn't fit the mould.

Soraya lifted her chin. 'I'm tinkering with the car. Hortense had trouble with it and I thought I'd take a look.'

'Hortense?' Zahir rubbed his chin ruminatively and Soraya almost thought she heard the whisper of early-morning bristles against his hand. His chin was shadowed, accentuating the proud angle of his jaw.

'The housekeeper,' Soraya explained. 'She can take another vehicle.' She waved towards the new models filling the rest of the garage. 'But she's used to this one.'

'You don't have to do that. You're a guest.'

'But I *enjoy* it.' Soraya braced herself for a look of dismay or disapproval.

Instead she was rewarded with a grin that kicked her pulse to top speed.

'Better you than me, Soraya. Horses, people or computers I'll willingly spend hours with. But the underside of a chassis? You can have it and welcome.'

Warmth curled round Soraya's heart and squeezed hard. Zahir's eyes danced and she felt her mouth tilt in an answering smile.

'Yet you drive like a professional.' She loved sitting beside Zahir as he drove them through the countryside. He was competent; not afraid of speed, but she'd never felt in safer hands.

'That's because I *am* a professional. I was trained by the best. Defensive driving, off-road navigation and dune-driving for starters.'

He slung his towel casually over one shoulder, not bothering to wipe away the stray droplets of water that ran from his hair down his collarbone. Soraya followed their progress over his burnished flesh and found herself clasping her hands together far too tightly.

'I can strip down a motor and get it back together in record time,' he continued, oblivious to her stare. 'But that doesn't mean I'd do it for fun.'

'What *do* you do for fun? How do you relax?'

Zahir's easy smile faded.

'You must do something to unwind,' she persevered.

'I find ways.' His voice dropped so low it plucked at her nerve ends and made her tremble.

Green fire blazed beneath his now-hooded lids and Soraya felt an answering conflagration start somewhere in her midriff. As his eyes held hers that ball of heat plunged down to her pelvis. The thud of her heartbeat swelled to a roar that clogged her senses.

Women, she realised. He relaxed with *women*.

The sexual awareness in his stare was so blatant even someone as inexperienced as she couldn't miss it.

But he wasn't thinking about other women now.

Zahir was looking at *her*.

That look was a caress, trailing across her skin and drawing every muscle and nerve ending into singing life.

Soraya revelled in it. Gone in an instant was a lifetime's caution, obliterated by a welling force so elemental it muted any opposition.

Suddenly that tension, the unspoken awareness they'd tried to pretend didn't exist, was back full force. Soraya had tried to convince herself she'd imagined it. Now she saw it in Zahir's intense look. Its impact dragged the air from her lungs.

Did she look at him the same way?

The air between them shimmered as if with heat haze. Honeyed warmth pooled low between her legs and a strange lethargy stole through her.

If Zahir were to close the space between them and reach out his hand she'd welcome his touch.

She *willed* him to do it.

His eyes dropped to her mouth and her lips throbbed as if in response to the brush of his mouth against hers.

What would his kiss be like? Urgent and fiery or slow and sensuous?

Soraya's eyelids drooped as if weighted. Her lips opened, ripe for his. Her hands slipped from where they'd looped around her legs. Her chest rose as a fractured breath became a sigh of expectation.

Zahir stepped close, so close she felt a drop of pool water land on her ankle. She looked up, stretching her neck to hold his gaze.

Did she imagine a tremor pass through his solid frame?

'I...' He speared a hand through his hair. 'I have a meeting in Paris,' he said finally, his voice harsh. 'I won't be back for dinner. Don't wait up for me.'

A moment later he was gone.

A day alone had done nothing to douse the flare of sexual excitement smouldering within her.

Soraya was honest enough not to pretend it was anything

else that made her skin seem too tight for her body and her pulse points ache with longing.

It was an awful irony that now, mere weeks from going to the man she had to marry, she was finally experiencing sexual desire. A desire she'd believed herself immune to.

That didn't mean she had to give in to it. She'd busied herself, thinking if she kept herself occupied every minute of every day until her return to Bakhara she'd conquer this yearning.

It hadn't worked so far—despite tuning the four-wheel drive till it purred, putting in hours on the laptop finishing her report, catching up on emails, driving to a local market and stocking up on so much mouth-watering fresh produce poor Hortense had been cooking all afternoon.

Now, as the day drew to a close and Zahir hadn't returned, Soraya knew she couldn't settle with a book or film.

What better time to face what she'd been putting off ever since they'd arrived?

She took a deep breath and walked down the first step into the outdoor pool. The water was like warm silk on her feet and ankles, yet goose bumps broke out on Soraya's flesh.

Another step and she tried to concentrate on how the underwater lights made the depths look appealing, the blue and gold key-pattern mosaic that ran the sides of the pool.

Her pulse revved as she moved deeper. But her hand was firm on the sun-warmed flagstone at the pool edge. She had nothing to fear, she reminded herself.

Only the fear she'd never been able to conquer.

Her brain filled with the image of that toddler, ghastly pale as Zahir hauled him from the stream. Her stomach twisted and terror was sharp metal on her tongue.

Had she looked like that the day she'd almost drowned?

This time she was determined to conquer her phobia.

Finally she reached a point where she couldn't proceed without submerging. Her heart hammered but she made herself turn and grip the edge with both trembling hands.

Her legs stretched out, weightless behind her. Soraya was

torn between a thrill of exhilaration that she'd ventured so far beyond her comfort zone, and crawling horror at what might happen next.

Experimentally she kicked her legs. It was easier than she'd expected. But how to coordinate arms and legs? Better to concentrate on floating.

It took a while but finally she let go with one arm. If she could just relax enough she was sure she could float. Everyone said it was so easy. Daringly, she let her body stretch out, till she gripped the edge by her fingertips. See? It wasn't so hard. Tomorrow she'd go to the shallow end and try it without holding on. She'd…

'Soraya?' Out of the dusk a figure loomed.

She opened her mouth to reply and swallowed water. Shock swamped her. She scrabbled for the edge, one arm flailing even as she went under.

Panic welled, fed by the taste of treated water in her mouth and nostrils. Shock gave way to fear and she thrashed for the surface.

Till strong arms hauled her up, holding her tight.

She clawed at wide shoulders, desperate for the feel of solid bone and flesh beneath her fingers. Precious oxygen filled her lungs and she gulped it down in great, gasping breaths.

'It's okay, Soraya. You're all right. You're safe. I've got you.' Zahir's voice, like dark treacle, seeped past the panic, finally slowing her frantic heartbeat.

Eyes smarting, she wrapped her arms tight round his neck, burying her face against Zahir's slick skin. He felt warm and solid and so very, very safe.

'But who's got you?' she gasped. 'The water's too deep to stand.' Her lips moved against his skin and she tasted male spice and salt, but she couldn't bring herself to lift her head away.

'I've got us both. Don't worry.'

She registered his big hands splayed warm around her ribs. His legs moved against hers, slowly kicking as he kept them afloat.

'You're sure?' She hated how unsteady she sounded.

'Positive.'

A moment later she felt the tiled steps beneath her feet. His hand uncurled hers from their vice-like grip of his neck and placed it on the warm flagstone at the pool's edge.

'You're safe now. Absolutely.'

Yet it wasn't the stairs beneath her feet that convinced her. It was Zahir's strong, hard form flush against hers.

She'd assumed the next time they met she'd feel awkward, remembering the sizzle of sexual awareness that had charged the atmosphere back in the garage. But embarrassment was obliterated by relief.

'Thank you.' She couldn't seem to let him go, but clung to him with her other arm, her heart galloping. He seemed to understand, for he didn't release her.

'You don't swim?' His eyes held hers.

She shook her head. 'No,' she croaked.

'And you were in the pool because...?'

'I was teaching myself to float.' Her mouth wobbled in a parody of a smile. 'Or trying to.' She clamped her lips shut, not wanting to go further. Yet his constant, silent regard finally dragged the truth from her. 'I'm scared of the water.'

She waited for his look of surprise but it didn't come. He merely nodded his head. 'Sensible of you. I would be too if I couldn't swim.'

A ribbon of heat unfurled within her at Zahir's easy acceptance and matter-of-fact tone. No condescension, no disbelief. He said nothing more, just held her safe as the water lapped around them and Soraya was grateful for his silent support.

'It was the boy,' she finally said, needing to explain. 'Seeing him almost die because he couldn't save himself.' She yanked in a breath. 'I saw him and felt...'

She looked away. What had she felt? Horror, déjà vu, fear. *And more.*

'I felt ashamed I'd never conquered my fear and learned to swim. I don't want to be that helpless.'

Zahir's fingers tightened on her. 'Why are you so scared of the water?'

'I almost drowned as a child. I was playing in the shallows. I thought my mother was watching me but she was…busy.'

Soraya pulled in a searing breath. Her mother had gone to her lover, the man she had eventually ran away with, presumably thinking Soraya wouldn't venture deep.

Somehow through the years the two events had become entangled in her brain—the loss of her mother and her brush with death. As a child she'd almost believed she'd somehow driven her mother to leave with her near-drowning. Of course she knew better now, but the result was a dread of water she'd never been able to overcome.

Zahir's broad palm slid up her back then down again in a gesture of silent comfort that unstrung more of the tension still threading her body.

'What happened in Amboise must have brought it all back for you. No wonder you were white as a sheet.'

Soraya shrugged stiffly. 'It was…horrible. But it made me realise I couldn't go on pretending this fear doesn't matter. I have to do something about it.'

Strong fingers took her chin and lifted it till she was staring into eyes dark as the night closing in around them.

'Promise me you won't do it alone.' Though soft, Zahir's voice had a rough edge that abraded her senses.

'But I—'

'I'll teach you to swim, Soraya. Just promise me you won't try it alone.'

Her heart pounded as his gaze held hers. Soraya's insides melted at the banked heat she saw there.

'I promise.'

'Good.' He nodded and took her hand in his. 'We'll start now.'

'Now?' Her eyes rounded.

'No time like the present. Besides, we don't want tonight's episode to compound your fear, do we?'

It already had, but she bit down on the admission. The thought of going further into the depths horrified her.

Zahir's fingers threaded between hers, his strength and heat melding with hers.

'Trust me, Soraya?'

Her gaze roved his serious, almost grim face. She took in the lines of strength and character carved beside his mouth. There was determination in that solid jaw, arrogance in those aristocratic cheekbones and imperious nose, and a question in his clear gaze.

She thought of all she knew of him. He was capable, dependable and kind. How could she not trust him?

'Yes,' she said finally, and let him draw her into the water.

'Tilt your head back into the water further.'

Soraya did as he bid and Zahir was amazed anew that this was the same woman who a short time ago had been thrashing in panic half a metre from the edge of the pool. Now she floated on her back, his hands beneath her, the safeguard she needed to be confident in the water.

It humbled him that she trusted him so implicitly. Particularly since trust hadn't come easily to her. Initially they'd been like wary, armed combatants in an uneasy truce because of his early misjudgements of her.

Recently that wariness had blossomed into something akin to friendship, or at least understanding.

Except when his libido escaped his constraints and reminded him she was the most seductively attractive woman he'd ever known. Dancing with her in a public square had tested his limits. But this… Even dressed in a tank top and cut-offs rather than a skimpy bikini, she fired his blood.

'Why didn't you wear a swimsuit?' He asked, trying to take his mind off the sensual promise of her body spread before him.

He felt like a sultan offered a feast for the senses. But he had to deny himself and keep his touch brisk and businesslike. He couldn't betray her trust.

'I don't own one.' She darted a look at him then away. 'There's no point when I'd never use it.'

Zahir refrained from pointing out many women wore bikinis that never got wet. They were for display, to show off ripe female curves to best advantage.

The more he knew Soraya the more he understood she was unique. Her shame at not overcoming her fear had surprised him. Her determination to beat it rather than live with what she saw as weakness appealed. She was some woman.

He applauded her pride and perseverance. She had such heart—as much as any warrior he'd known.

Yet her bravery had run close to stupidity tonight. In an instant she'd shattered the hard-won calm he'd spent all day working to achieve. What if he hadn't come down to the pool for a swim? What if she'd drowned here alone? Anger and fear vied for dominance.

'What were you doing in the deep end?' Despite his best efforts his voice had a raw edge.

'I knew if I was in the shallows I wouldn't push myself. I had to face the danger.'

Hot shivers rippled through Zahir's belly. 'Just don't do it again, *ever*, without me.'

She drove him crazy. Pride, fear and desire made for a combustible mix. How much longer could he keep a lid on them all?

'I've already promised I won't.' She looked at him solemnly and his heart kicked against his ribs. 'But I need to learn fast. You won't always be around to help me.'

Of course he wouldn't. He'd be managing Bakhara's largest province and Soraya would be…with Hussein.

Clammy sweat broke out on Zahir's skin and sick dread churned his stomach. He tried so hard to be honourable in thought as well as deed, but lately it was more than he could do.

It was a constant battle to rein in his imagination. As for concentrating on teaching her to relax in the water—it took every ounce of determination to focus.

'Try kicking again but keep your legs straight.'

She did as instructed and together they moved down the pool.
'I'm moving! I'm swimming!'

The delighted look she sent him drove a shaft of pure pleasure through his chest.

It was more reward than he deserved.

Even as he smiled back, his body tensed.

Her long hair, unbound for the first time, spread in a cloud
of dark satin. Like mermaid's tresses it caressed his hands,
arms and belly as he walked with her. He'd never imagined it
was so long. Now he couldn't help but wonder what it would
be like rippling down her naked back and breasts as he made
love to her.

Unable to take any more, he slipped his hands from beneath
her and moved just far enough away to avoid contact. They
were in the shallow end and she was in no danger.

Excited at her success, she didn't notice his withdrawal. Her
face glowed with effervescent joy.

A man would have to be made of desert stone not to respond to Soraya.

Despite his reputation as a hard warrior, Zahir was made of
all-too-human flesh. If only he *were* stone!

How could he hold out against a woman who appealed to
him on a level no woman ever had? Not even the girl he'd been
head over heels in love with as a youth.

'Zahir? What's wrong?' She was standing, water sluicing
down the black top that clung like a second skin.

He shook his head. 'Nothing's wrong.' He turned away.
'That's enough now. We'll continue tomorrow and you can
learn to float face-down, ready to swim properly.'

'Really?' She caught his hand and stopped him moving
away. 'You think I'm ready?'

Reluctantly he turned and looked down into a face that to
his dazzled eyes seemed flawless. Excitement shone in her eyes
and her smile wrapped around his heart.

He wasn't aware of reaching out but found his hand cupping

her jaw. Her satiny skin was smooth and sleek to the touch. Her pulse trembled against his fingertips.

Something deep inside, something stronger than logic or caution, roared into life.

Her eyes were wide as she swayed towards him, her lips parting. To warn him off?

It was too late.

His lips met hers and the world collapsed around them.

CHAPTER NINE

SORAYA had imagined his kiss so often. She'd even dreamed of it. The reality obliterated her imaginings as a tidal wave would the ripple of a single stone.

Zahir's broad hands cradled her face, his touch tender yet strong as he held her head just so and angled his own for better access.

His questing tongue slicked her lips, parted them, and she shuddered in great racking waves as sensation exploded within her. Zahir devoured her, invited her, stole her breath with his audacious demands, yet even while plundering rapaciously offered back such sweet, poignant pleasure Soraya was lost.

The fresh taste of his breath was in her mouth. It was the most delicious flavour in the world—spice and salt and the mystery that was maleness. His scent filled her nostrils. His hard body was muscled and intriguing, his heart thundering with hers. His wet skin burned, branding her through her clothes, making her breasts tingle and a curl of indescribable tension twist deep and low.

Instinctively she grabbed his shoulders, swaying as her limbs melted, and the world became a place she didn't recognise.

Nothing had prepared her for the vital life force throbbing through them as if they were one. Or the need spiralling out of control and the sheer wanton delight of being in his arms. Every sense was hyper-alert. Even the softly eddying water was a silken caress drawing her deeper into sensual overload.

She'd never felt more frail, more delicately feminine than now, with his heavy-muscled thighs braced wide around her, his hands trapping her, and his mouth seducing her with sheer, carnal pleasure.

Yet she'd never felt stronger. As if power sizzled and sparked in her blood. As if she could lay mountains low with a single flick of her fingers.

His kiss shattered her and rebuilt her at the same time.

Her hands slid from his shoulders to the back of his neck, up through his damp hair and he growled low in the back of his throat. It was a sound of approval, of male possession, and she revelled in it. Revelled in the power that she, even with her inexperience, had over this man who haunted her thoughts and dreams.

His tongue slid against hers, demanding a response, and she gave it, tentatively at first, then wholeheartedly, lost in the wonder of this heady world of passion.

Her whole body ached, throbbed for Zahir. Only him. She wanted to climb up his tall frame and meld herself against him. She *needed* with a desperation she'd never experienced or thought to know.

Even the rough pressure of his chest expanding against hers incited a thrill.

Soraya pressed closer, needy as never before. She loved the feel of his body, the unfamiliar outline of muscle, bone and sinew. The tickle of his hairy legs against hers. Lifting herself higher into his hold, her hips tilted against him and she registered the solid proof of his arousal.

At the feel of him, hot and heavy just *there* against her, she stilled. A frayed thread of common sense told her to move away, yet some older, sense-deep feminine instinct urged her closer.

Soraya was swaying nearer when firm hands grabbed her upper arms. An instant later she gulped huge drafts of air into oxygen-starved lungs as he put her from him. But nothing made up for the loss of Zahir's mouth on hers, or his body against hers.

Hungrily she eyed his reddened lips. They were drawn flat now, matching the horizontal lines furrowing his brow.

Yet his eyes didn't match his scowl. His eyes were smoky-dark and held a hint of the same shock she felt.

Soraya loved his eyes, she realised. From the first when they'd watched her so intently she'd felt a sizzle of awareness. Even when he'd looked askance at her, Zahir's eyes had fascinated. Now they shared the secret she felt: the secret turmoil of amazing emotions and sensations.

The secret his grim face denied.

'I'm sorry.' His voice was harsh and unrecognisable. 'That shouldn't have happened.'

His gaze left hers to fix on something over her shoulder. As if he couldn't bear to see her. Or as if he couldn't face what he read in her face.

It was the first time he'd ever avoided her gaze.

Soraya felt something crumble inside.

She gulped down a shaky breath and searched for control. Her heart pounded and she had the shakes so badly she wasn't sure she could stand without his support.

'But you can't pretend it didn't happen.' The words emerged breathless and uneven.

She didn't understand what made her say it till he yanked his gaze back to hers and heat exploded inside.

That's why. Because you want to feel it again—what Zahir makes you feel.

Because you want him to admit he feels it too.

But Zahir shook his head, thrusting her further away.

'It was *wrong*.' The last word was dragged from him as if from a tortured soul and she felt his pain as hers. His hands dropped and he stepped back, as if unable to remain within touching distance.

As if she tainted him.

Of course it was wrong. Soraya understood that all too well. To desire her husband-to-be's most trusted advisor was disastrous. Unthinkable!

Yet it felt so right. When it was just she and Zahir, it felt incredible.

'Zahir. Please, I…'

She didn't know what she was going to say. Only knew she couldn't bear the pain she read on his proud features. That she had to ease it somehow.

Yet he didn't give her the chance. Before the words had left her mouth he'd vaulted from the pool, every line of his athlete's body taut with rejection.

He didn't say a word as he strode away.

Sunlight flooded the dining room as Soraya lingered over a very late breakfast. She'd fallen asleep at dawn and couldn't summon the energy to go out, despite the glorious day.

What had she done?

Her flesh prickled whenever she thought of last night's kiss. The way Zahir's body and hers had fused together, driven by a force so potent she'd had no chance of overcoming it.

Or had she?

She shivered and rubbed her hands up her arms.

Her life had been shaped by the mother who'd left when she was six. Her mother had flitted from one affair to another. First to Soraya's father, then to a string of handsome men till her untimely death.

Maybe it was a response to the negativity of those who expected her to turn out like her mum, but Soraya had never sought male attention. She'd happily accepted her beloved father's over-protective ways and steered clear of men.

She'd told herself love was a weakness and desire—

She pushed her untasted breakfast away.

Desire had been a mere word. Safe in the knowledge she'd never experienced it, Soraya had supposed she never would. Until Zahir had caught her in his stormy gaze and nothing had been the same. It was as if he'd branded her as his that night and nothing, not logic or the threat of approaching marriage, could change that.

Her heart dipped.

Was she too destined to make a fool of herself, of honour and duty, for an attractive man?

It didn't matter that duty led her down a path she shrank from. She'd committed to her fate. She couldn't change it. Soraya pressed a hand to her forehead, as if to still her whirling thoughts.

She should be ashamed she'd kissed Zahir and wanted more.

Yes, she felt guilt and horror at what she'd done. Yet that wasn't all. Last night had felt *right*, as if she and Zahir were *meant*. No matter how she castigated herself she couldn't regret that kiss. It was emblazoned in her soul. A single point of perfect happiness.

It did no good to tell herself it was more than sex. That she'd begun to fall for the proud, caring, fascinating man she'd come to know. That just made the situation more impossible.

'Mademoiselle?' Soraya looked up to see the housekeeper in the doorway. 'Monsieur El Hashem sent this for you.'

'Thank you, Hortense.' Puzzled, she took the shopping bag from her hand. Inside Soraya discovered silky material in swirling aquamarine and turquoise.

'*Monsieur* said he'd be waiting for you in the pool.'

'The pool?' Soraya's head shot up, tension crackling through her.

Hortense nodded and tsked as she collected Soraya's still-laden breakfast plate. 'That's right. He said you had a lesson.'

It was foolhardy, Zahir knew. Being alone with her, his hands on her body, would be purest temptation. Yet he'd promised to teach her to swim.

The memory of Soraya flailing in the water, panicking and possibly drowning but for his intervention, froze his veins with a glacial chill. He had to know she'd be safe.

Besides, it would be cowardly to back out. A woman with so much heart and character deserved his respect.

She didn't deserve his tongue in her mouth and his erection

surging between her legs—no matter how much he wanted her. She mightn't be a complete innocent but he'd taken her by surprise with his ardour. He'd felt her shock and tried to pull back. Instead he'd succumbed to pleasure so intense it was like a drug.

Sweat broke out on his brow as Zahir relived the intense pleasure of last night's kiss. The taste of her so deliciously enticing. The feel of her siren's body against his. That mix of sweet tenderness and fiery wanton that had blown him away.

The wanting had been bad enough before he'd touched her. After last night it would be pure torment, knowing paradise was so close yet so far beyond his reach.

A sound made him look up. Soraya walked towards the pool, closely wrapped in a voluminous towelling robe despite the heat. Even seeing her bundled up sent his pulse soaring. Her hair, almost to her waist, trailed over one shoulder like an invitation to touch. Even her bare feet were enticing.

Zahir swallowed a knot of tension.

This would be his penance. Every second would be torture but he deserved it, and worse.

She was Hussein's woman. He'd known it and still hadn't stopped. Now he would face his punishment though it would be the most difficult thing he'd ever done.

She stopped by the pool, eyes wary.

'Are you sure you want to do this?'

'I promised I would teach you to swim. I never go back on a promise.' Yet just watching her played havoc with his breathing. A tremor quivered through his limbs as he met her doubtful gaze.

'I apologise for my behaviour last night.' The words spilled from stiff lips. 'I have no excuse. But, believe me, it won't happen again.'

She met his eyes and for an insane moment he felt a thud of connection between them. It made no difference. It *couldn't* make a difference.

'I'm sorry too,' she murmured, her gaze dipping. 'Last night… It wasn't just you. It was me too.'

Zahir didn't need to be reminded of how she'd undone him with her sweet responsiveness. He shook his head. He knew exactly where the guilt lay.

'I'm responsible for you.'

'For my safety. That's all.' Her eyes sparkled with a militant light but he forbore to argue.

'Thank you for the swimsuit,' she said at last, not quite meeting his gaze. 'You must have been out early.'

He hadn't been to bed, had spent the night alternately berating himself and reliving the guilty pleasure he'd sworn to put behind him.

Zahir remained silent as she fumbled with the tie at her waist and let the robe fall away.

The air sucked from his lungs in a rush as she turned.

She looked like a mermaid, indecently alluring even in the most modest one-piece outfit he could find. He'd been right about her size—too right. The stretch fabric clung like a lover's caress, making his fingers itch as he remembered the feel of her beneath his hands.

She was all enticing curves and supple limbs. The fall of her hair in thick, waving tresses accentuated her femininity, appealing to some primal male part of him that relished each difference between them. Heat roared through him in an out-of-control rush and he fought to retain his composure.

Deliberately he looked at his watch. 'We've just time for another lesson before we leave.'

She faltered at the edge of the pool. 'Leave?'

Zahir nodded and beckoned her down the steps. 'Yes. I've arranged the next leg of our journey. You wanted to see France and you can't do that while we're isolated here.'

He looked away before he could read her reaction. It didn't matter what she said; the decision was made. Immersion in rural quiet had thrown them together. What they needed now was people, cities, action. Anything to keep them occupied and stop him dwelling on Soraya Karim and what she did to him.

Half an hour later Soraya was flushed with excitement and pleasure at what she'd achieved. Even her distress and embarrassment had ebbed to a dull, gnawing ache. For Zahir was utterly businesslike, intent only on her progress.

It was as if last night hadn't happened, except for the jerk of electricity, as if from a live wire, whenever they touched.

Now, breathless, she sank back against the end of the pool, watching as Zahir hauled himself out.

The play of bunching muscles across his back and arms mesmerised her. He really was the most remarkable-looking man. She could watch him for hours. Every movement was graceful despite the raw power he so carefully leashed.

'What's that mark? The one along your side?'

As he turned, his brows jammed together as if he was displeased she'd ended their unspoken agreement to avoid personal topics.

'I've been a warrior all my life. I have scars. It comes with the territory.' He shrugged and reached for his towel.

Soraya noticed then that the dark golden skin of his back was smooth and unblemished. The old scars were on his chest and arms. The marks of a warrior.

Something, a little frisson of feminine excitement, tingled through her, making her frown. It wasn't that she relished the idea of combat, but at a deep, primitive level there was something thrilling about the idea of a strong man prepared to defend what he believed in.

'But that one's different.' She pointed to a white pucker of flesh at his side. It was none of her business but she couldn't stifle the need to know more about him. Surely her question was innocuous?

Sighing, he rubbed the towel over his face. 'A bullet caught me.'

Soraya's breath hitched in a hiss of dismay. Her heart hammered at the thought of Zahir in a gun's sights.

'It's okay, Soraya.' He must have read her horror, for his severe expression eased. 'It was just a flesh wound and a bit of a knick to one rib.'

Just a knick...

'How did it happen?' Prying or not, she couldn't leave it there.

'I used to lead the Emir's personal protection unit, remember? I came between him and someone who intended harm.'

Soraya clung to the side of the pool as weakness invaded her limbs. Zahir had put himself in front of the Emir. Taken a bullet meant for him!

Slowly she shook her head. 'I can't comprehend how you could do that. Put yourself in danger that way.'

'Can't you?' Eyes of vivid emerald caught and held hers. 'Isn't there anyone you'd risk yourself for?'

Before she could answer he went on, 'It was my job. What I'd signed on to do. More than that, Hussein is far more than an employer to me.'

The ripple of emotion across his stern features surprised her. 'Hussein was the one who rescued me from my father's palace when I was just a child. As supreme leader he forced my father's hand into letting me go. Not that my father was bothered about keeping me.' Zahir's austerely sculpted lips curled in a smile that held no humour. It sent a terrible chill prickling down Soraya's spine. What did he mean, his father hadn't been bothered about keeping him?

'Hussein has been father and friend to me. Mentor and role model. I don't just owe him my job, but my life. If I'd stayed in my father's palace I've no doubt I'd have died from neglect.'

The quiet certainty in Zahir's calm tone turned Soraya's blood cold. He'd said his early years were eventful but she'd had no idea.

'What about your mother?'

Absently he swiped his towel over his shoulders. 'I never knew her. She died when I was tiny. So there was no-one to care that I ran feral, barely surviving. No-one to care that my father never legally acknowledged me as his.'

'Zahir!' Having grown up with at least one loving parent, Soraya found the picture he painted appalling. She could barely imagine being so alone.

He shrugged. 'They weren't married. She was one of his mistresses. A dancing girl. Why should he stir himself over a brat who wasn't even legitimately his?' His tone was blank, as if his father's rejection didn't bother him.

How could that be? Soraya knew too well the weight a parent's rejection. She'd carried it ever since she was six. What hidden scars burdened Zahir? It must have been doubly painful for him not to have either parent there for him when he was young.

She'd seen behind Zahir's mask of calm. She knew beyond the formidable control was a man of powerful emotions and blazing passion. A man who felt deeply.

The memory of that man sent heat spiralling in that secret feminine place.

'Hussein gave me a home.' Zahir's voice deepened to that low burr that brushed the back of her neck into tingling heat. 'He cared about me, raised me, made me who I am. I owe him everything, especially loyalty.' Zahir paced the edge of the pool towards her, his words ringing between them, deliberate and measured.

'I could never betray him.'

He was reminding her why there could never be anything between them, despite the shimmering heat that charged the air and the growing sense of a bond between them. Zahir was a man of honour and loyalty. How much more loyal could you get than to offer your life to save another?

No wonder he'd looked sick last night as he'd turned from her. By kissing her, he'd betrayed the man he'd admired all his life.

Against that, the guilt that hounded her paled. To her the Emir was a distant benefactor. How much worse this all was for Zahir, who knew and loved him.

Her heart twisted for Zahir. For the pain he'd borne in the past. For the hurt she'd unwittingly caused him.

And for herself, trapped between duty and desire, with no way out. Her throat closed convulsively. Was that all the future held? Duty?

Once she'd believed it would be enough. She'd thought emotional independence was all she needed.

Then recently she'd begun to imagine a future other than the one mapped out for her—a future of her own making, where she could pursue the half-formed hopes and dreams she'd dared to dream in Paris. Of a career, a future that was about *her* needs and interests, not the nation's.

Now even that seemed unreal, unsatisfactory, a poor facsimile of a *real* future. For the first time in her life Soraya caught a glimpse of what life might be like with more than solely career or duty to fill it. With a man she cared for, a man who made her blood spark and her soul take flight. A man like Zahir...

Like a tidal wave, realisation crashed down on her. She grabbed for the edge of the pool, desperate for support as her world reeled.

'Time to move. We're leaving here, and remember you need to pack.' Zahir turned his back rather than let his gaze run over her again.

The swimming lesson had been as testing as he'd feared. Even the mention of what he owed Hussein only succeeded in racheting up the level of sick guilt in his belly. It did nothing to drive out his fascination with Soraya. It was as if she'd got under his skin, like a desert sandstorm infiltrating every defence.

What *was* it about Soraya? Even in the throes of first love he hadn't felt so...saturated by his feelings. They impinged on every thought after years of him bottling them up. He was aware of her as if she was part of him. Nor was it simple sexual awareness. If only it were that!

He slung the towel round his neck then shot a glance over her shoulder.

She hadn't moved. She stood, hands braced on the flagstones at the edge of the pool, head bent as if winded.

'Soraya?' Concern spiked. He turned back to her. She didn't look up, and he saw her breasts rise and fall quickly as if she'd just swum a sprint. He yanked his gaze higher and realised her face was pale.

He'd thought it impossible to feel more guilt, but he'd been wrong. The way she stood, as if absorbing a body blow, told him she battled pain. Because of him? His chest constricted hard.

Disregarding his resolution not to touch her again, he extended his hand. 'Come on, princess. It's time we left.'

'I told you before—*don't* call me that!'

Zahir's blood frosted as she looked up and he read the haunted depths of her eyes. The slight shadows that spoke of a sleepless night were more pronounced in her milky-white face. Her skin looked drawn too tight. Even her lush mouth seemed pinched.

'Soraya?' His scalp itched with warning. Something was very wrong. 'What is it?'

She shook her head and looked away.

'Sorry,' she mumbled. 'It's nothing. I overreacted.'

Zahir's brow knotted. Even in the face of his blatant disapproval she'd stood defiant and proud. Yet now she looked as if the merest breeze would knock her down.

'Because I called you princess?'

She gave no response, ignoring his hand and clambering stiffly from the pool. Yet even in the sun she shivered, and he draped his towel around her. It said something about her state of mind that she stood meekly while he wrapped it close, rubbing her arms through the towelling.

'Soraya?' She met his gaze but her eyes had a dazed, blind look that worried him. 'What is it?'

'Nothing. I'm fine.' He refused to move away. Finally she spoke again. 'My mother used to call me that, you know.' Her lips stretched in a parody of a smile. 'When I was tiny I even used to believe I was a little princess. At least that I was *her* princess.'

The towel slipped and she clutched it close.

'It just goes to show how gullible children are, doesn't it?' Her voice rang hollow. 'I wasn't special enough to make her stay when her latest lover called. She left me behind then without a second thought.'

A shudder racked her and Zahir had to fight the need to tug her close and wrap himself around her. She looked…fragile.

But a moment later Soraya recovered. She straightened, pushing her shoulders back in that familiar way and turned to survey the pool.

'The last time she called me that was the day I almost drowned. I was wading in a pool and I was sure she was still there, watching me. I didn't find out till later that was the day she'd left us to go to her lover.'

His heart wrenched at the pain he read in her taut features. At the hurt she battled even to think of venturing into water again. He'd believed her strong and determined but he hadn't known the half of it.

'I should have remembered that lesson,' she murmured.

'What lesson?'

'Never to expect too much.' Her expression held infinite sadness as she turned and walked away.

Zahir felt as if someone had taken a knife to his belly and gutted him.

CHAPTER TEN

SORAYA leaned on the railing of the giant motor cruiser and took in the brilliant cluster of lights that was Monte Carlo. Even the water was gold and silver, reflecting the illuminated city climbing the hills.

All around her was luxury. From the multi-million-dollar vessels crammed into the marina to the exclusive party she'd left on the other deck.

Was this what her life would be like as the Emir's wife? A world of untold wealth and privilege?

Fervently she wished she could be thrilled by the prospect. Another woman might have found nothing but pleasure in the comforts of extreme wealth but Soraya had so much on her mind, they left her unmoved. They were comforts Zahir took for granted, fitting easily into this rarefied world of diplomats, royalty and celebrities.

He might have been a bodyguard once, and a lost soul as a child, but he'd moved on. He was strong, confident, a man sure of himself and his purpose, with nothing to prove.

Her heart squeezed haphazardly as she thought of her weeks with Zahir. Despite the caution they exercised, she'd slipped further under his spell.

Riding horses in the Camargue, eating heavenly bouilla-baisse in a tiny waterfront restaurant, even visiting lavender fields and a perfume factory; Soraya couldn't have asked for a better companion. He'd been pleasant, amusing and caring.

Yet he scrupulously kept a telling distance between them. He hadn't touched her again. Even during her swimming lessons, and he insisted on those daily. He supervised, instructed and encouraged but kept to the side of the pool.

How she missed his touch! His strong arms around her.

A sigh shuddered through her.

She couldn't ask for more. Briefly she'd been angry at his unswerving loyalty to the Emir, for it meant there was no chance for *them*. But there *was* no 'them'. There were too many obstacles against it. Besides, Zahir's loyalty was part of what made him the man he was.

All she could do was store up memories against a future when he must be a stranger to her. That was what she'd done, gathered memories, as if they could comfort her when she gave herself to another man.

She'd railed at a fate that bound her to a marriage she didn't want. How much worse now when, too late, she'd discovered what it was to care deeply? *For the wrong man.*

Pain tore through her and she gripped the railing harder. She wanted…

No! She couldn't allow herself to go there.

That morning of her second swimming lesson Zahir had thought her upset because he'd called her 'princess'.

It was true the casual endearment had evoked painful memories. But the real anguish had come from the realization that she, who'd thought herself immune from love, had fallen for a man who could never be hers.

She was head over heels in love with Zahir.

The knowledge made her body sing with excitement and her soul shrivel. It was wonderful, delicious and terrible. A blessing that was a curse.

Travelling with him was torture and pleasure combined. Maybe if he felt nothing for her it would be easier, but his punctilious distance told her he felt something for her too. That knowledge kept her on a knife edge of torment, trawling back through conversations, seeking proof of his feelings. Like

Bastille Day, when he'd asked about the possibility of her loving someone other than her betrothed.

If only circumstances had been different.

'Soraya. What are you doing down here when the party's in full swing upstairs?'

Zahir halted several paces away. His eyes ate her up; she was luscious in a long dress of dusky rose. A gown that was innocently demure by the standards of the scantily dressed socialites at the party. Yet it skimmed her body in a way that reminded him too clearly of the hour-glass figure that tempted him during each day's swimming lesson.

Heat clutched deep in his belly.

Her scent, wildflowers rather than hothouse exotics, teased his nostrils. Her hair, held back by jewelled clips, cascaded down her back in a ripple of thick silk.

More than one man had cast covetous eyes on her tonight and Zahir had been busy staking a possessive claim on her to prevent any untoward advances.

Staking a claim on behalf of Hussein, he reminded himself.

She half-turned but didn't meet his eyes. 'I wanted some peace and quiet.'

At her words he stiffened. He'd seen her excited, happy, indignant and angry, but never listless.

There'd been inevitable tension after their kiss. But he'd worked hard not to let her see that taste of her had driven him to the brink of endurance. For her part, Soraya had thrown herself into sightseeing with a fervour that gave no hint she wanted anything else.

At first he'd wondered if she was a little too enthusiastic, then chided himself. It wasn't that he *wanted* her pining for what could never be.

'You're not enjoying yourself?' Tonight he'd sought safety in numbers. This exclusive society party had seemed a perfect alternative to a night alone with Soraya and the terrible gnawing tension within.

Beautiful women with come-hither eyes and smiles that

promised pleasure were here tonight in droves. Yet none had drawn a second glance from him.

Not one could hold a candle to Soraya for beauty or character. She was gentle—despite her bravado in standing up for herself—capable, caring, inquisitive and deeply fascinating. Her fierce independence, her determination and natural exuberance, entranced him. With her he'd felt more than he had in a decade and a half. It was like emerging from a grey half-life into a world of sunshine and colour.

'The party is amazing. Thank you for bringing me.' Yet she didn't sound as enthusiastic as when she discussed her research project. 'So many interesting people. So many celebrities. And I've never seen so much bling in my life.'

'But?'

She shook her head and those long tresses slid and curled around her slim back. Was it ridiculous to resent the fact she wore her hair down tonight? He hated the way men looked at her, imagining that bountiful hair loose around her shoulders as she made love.

He knew they did. Any man would.

He did. God help him!

'But it's only days till our flight from Rome to Bakhara.' Her husky words drew his belly tight. 'It's crept up on me and I needed time to digest it.'

She was going home to marry the finest man he knew.

Zahir ignored the wave of nausea that passed through him at the thought.

'I know Hussein is looking forward to seeing you.' If Hussein had any idea of the lovely woman she'd become, he'd be eager for her arrival.

Soraya bowed her head as if in assent. But her grip on the railing reminded him of a falcon's claws clamped hard and sharp on a leather glove.

'Soraya?' He took a pace towards her then, realising, stopped. '*Are* you all right?'

'Of course.' She tilted her chin up as she stared across the shimmering brightness. 'What could be wrong?'

Something was. He'd come to recognise the way she angled that neat chin as a defence mechanism.

He reminded himself his duty was simply to return her safe to Bakhara, not delve into her thoughts and fears.

Yet telling himself couldn't make it so. Nor could he banish the suspicion he knew *exactly* what was wrong. That, despite her proud front, Soraya felt as he did. That they'd circled an unspoken truth for weeks.

'Tell me!'

Perhaps the harshness in his voice surprised her for she turned her head, eyes wide and it was there again, that jangle along the senses as if lightning had sparked between them.

Damn it. He shouldn't feel this. He shouldn't feel anything except impersonal concern for her wellbeing.

Yet what he felt was personal. Far too personal.

Did she feel it too? Was that why she whipped her head round so fast?

'Soraya. Please.' It was no good telling himself this was merely a job. It had ceased to be 'just a job' the moment he had seen her in that Paris nightclub.

'I don't want to go back,' she said at last. 'I don't want...' Her voice dipped and she swallowed convulsively. That single movement spoke of a vulnerability that tugged at something in his very core. Something he couldn't name.

He found himself behind her, not touching, but mirroring her body with his as if to protect her. He couldn't keep back.

'What don't you want, Soraya?' His breath held.

A deep breath lifted her narrow shoulders. 'I don't want to marry the Emir.'

Like the boom of a bomb blast, her words rocked him back on his heels.

Elation ripped through him, a momentary inward cry of delight, till he smothered it, using every particle of will-power left to him.

It was on the tip of his tongue to ask why she didn't want to marry Hussein. But he wouldn't let the words come. He knew what he wanted her answer to be and he couldn't let either of them go there.

To betray Hussein would make him no better than his traitor father. And it would bring her nothing but shame and public disgrace.

His body snapped taut almost to breaking point. His chest rose and fell hard as he dragged in one sharp breath after another. Silence welled. One wrong word could shatter the world in a way that could never be repaired. The air around them strung close with tension.

'Why marry him then?' He told himself it was time to remind them both that this was what she really wanted. She'd just temporarily lost sight of the fact.

'Because I promised,' she whispered. 'It's arranged.'

'And you can't go back on your word.' It wasn't a question, it was recognition that she, like him, had standards to live by. Zahir had never broken a vow. He knew the value of a promise—particularly a promise given to the man who'd made him who he was today.

If only that reminder could strengthen him now! Temptation was here before him, made flesh in a way that threatened everything he knew of himself.

'That's right. It's my duty to marry him.'

Duty. Another word that ruled Zahir's world.

Wasn't it duty that kept him standing here, his body a mere hand span from hers? That tiny distance represented a yawning chasm, cleaved by his conscience. No matter what he wanted, duty kept her safe from his touch.

Yet it didn't prevent him feeling her heat, scenting her skin and hair, hearing her shaky little inhalations of breath. Almost, he embraced her. He remembered the imprint of her soft body against his and his will-power frayed.

'I promised him and my father. I owe them so much and it's what they both want.'

But not what she wanted.

'Did your father coerce you into it?' The suspicion drove bile to the back of Zahir's throat. Hussein would never do such a thing, but perhaps her father would.

'No.' Her voice rang true. 'My father is a dear man. He would never force me.'

'Then why did you agree?' Zahir hated the plea that broke his voice, but he was past dissembling.

She turned around and suddenly they were just a kiss apart. He ordered himself to move back but his feet wouldn't obey. He shoved his hands deep in his trouser pockets rather than be tempted to touch.

Her beautiful oval face tilted up towards his.

'I was fourteen, Zahir.'

'So young?' He frowned. Despite the old customs of his people, such an early betrothal was no longer the norm.

What had Hussein been thinking? Zahir's heart skipped at the unpalatable suspicion Hussein had been attracted to a girl barely in her teens. But their long engagement countered that idea.

The arrangement was odd. Why hadn't Hussein chosen a woman closer to his own age? Why wait ten years to marry?

Unless the betrothal had been hastily arranged?

The constitution stipulated the Emir of Bakhara had to be married, a family man with the prospect of heirs. Fortunately for Hussein a formal betrothal was as binding as marriage and there'd been no-one eager to hurry him into a second marriage when his beloved first wife had died. Had he chosen an early betrothal to keep the balance of power while he came to terms with his widower status?

'And you wanted to be queen.'

Soraya shook her head. Traditional Bakhari chandelier earrings scintillated at her ear lobes, drawing his eye to her delicate ears and slender throat.

Zahir clenched his hands tight in his pockets rather than reach out and stroke that delicate skin.

'No,' she said slowly. 'Not particularly, though the royal glamour was very exciting. But after a while I saw possibilities. As the Emir's consort I could be useful. Help our people. Devote myself to good works.' Her mouth twisted wryly as if mocking her earlier self.

'There's nothing wrong with that.' It sounded laudable, if distant from a flesh-and-blood marriage.

'Of course there's not.' Abruptly she looked away. 'That's exactly what I tell myself now when I try to imagine the future.'

A future when she would be Hussein's bride. In Hussein's arms.

'So why agree to the marriage?' Zahir's voice was rough. 'For the money? The prestige?'

'Zahir!'

Her shock made him look down, to discover he held her arms in a vice-like grip. Instantly he eased his hold.

'I'm sorry.' Yet he couldn't let her go. The touch of her soft flesh made him war with himself. 'Why, Soraya?'

'Because he saved my father's life.' Her eyes were dark pools of stormy emotion that dragged him down. A self-destructive part of him wanted to dive into those depths and never surface again.

'How?'

It shouldn't surprise him. He had first-hand knowledge of Hussein's generous spirit. Not only had Hussein saved Zahir as a child, he'd never held his father's treachery against him, measuring him against his own deeds rather than the taint of his blood kin.

'My father had a kidney disease,' Soraya responded. 'He needed a transplant, but you know how long the waiting list is for donors.'

Zahir nodded. Organ donation was still new in Bakhara and convincing people to join a donor registry was an uphill battle.

'He would have died while waiting for a transplant.' A tremor passed through her. 'I was too young to donate to him, and he wouldn't give his permission for me to do it.'

Of course she'd wanted to do it. Why wasn't he surprised?

'But the Emir said he owed my father his throne and his life. Apparently years ago there'd been an uprising by several tribal leaders. They'd tried to unseat the Emir and put one of their own in his place.'

Zahir stiffened. 'I know. My father was one of them.' The words scalded his tongue.

'He was?' Her eyes roved his face as if searching for something. 'You're not very like him, are you?'

'What do you mean?' Even now his skin crawled at the knowledge that man's blood ran in his veins. 'You didn't know him.'

'I know *you*, Zahir.' The way she spoke his name was like a caress.

He was so besotted he was hearing things now. He should step back but couldn't shift his feet. As for lifting his hold on her arms—it was impossible!

'I know you're a man of honour. A man who takes his responsibilities seriously.' Her lips curved in a wistful smile. 'I also know you'd never neglect a child of yours.'

'Of course not.' His lips thinned as he thought of the work still to be done to protect the rights of children, and others needing help, in his province.

'Of course not.' She twisted her hands and suddenly it was she holding him, her fingers on his soft yet strong. Ripples of illicit pleasure radiated from her touch.

'I saw you with that toddler. You didn't just save him, you cradled him and comforted him till his mother was calm enough to hold him. Then you made sure all the others were okay too, especially the teenager who blamed herself for not noticing he'd gone. You were gentle and understanding.'

'Anyone would do the same.' His voice was threadbare, stretched tight by the feel of Soraya holding him so tenderly. How he'd longed for her touch.

He should move away.

'Not everyone. Especially when the child was promptly sick

everywhere.' Her smile as she met his eyes was beguiling. He felt its impact deep in his diaphragm. 'You're a natural with kids. You'd be wonderful with your own.'

Suddenly he didn't need to break her hold. She did it, wrapping her arms around herself, as if chilled despite the balmy evening.

He wanted to comfort her, knowing from her stricken expression she felt pain. But he didn't trust himself to hold her then let her go.

'Anyway,' she said briskly, looking at a point near his shoulder. 'When the uprising occurred, my father sided with the Emir. In fact, he was with him when the palace was stormed. He was injured protecting the Emir and apparently it was the sight of blood drawn in the royal council-room that shocked the more sensible leaders into negotiation. The Emir always said my dad saved his life as well as the peace of the nation.'

'I've heard the story. But I hadn't realised that was your father.'

Soraya lifted her shoulders. 'It was a long time ago and I don't think either of them like to talk about it. Later, when my father got sick, the Emir did something truly extraordinary.' Her pale face lifted and he saw a genuine smile there, like a beacon in the shadows. 'He gave a kidney to save my father.'

'I had no idea.' Zahir was stunned. It must have happened the year he'd been sent to study in the USA. 'They kept it very quiet. I've heard nothing about it.'

No wonder. For a nation's ruler to risk his wellbeing like that was almost incomprehensible. Zahir could think of no other who would do it. But Hussein was in a class of his own.

'It's easy to thank someone, but to repay a debt like that…' Soraya shook her head.

'He's a special man.' Zahir had known that since he was four.

'Yes.' Her dark eyes clung to his. 'He is. So when he asked for marriage, my father was thrilled. He knew I'd be marrying the very best of men.'

Zahir nodded, unable to fault her father's logic, even though thinking of her with Hussein made hot pincers tear at his innards.

'So you see,' she added in a low voice that tugged at him, 'I have every reason to marry him and none to refuse.'

'Except you don't love him.'

Her eyes widened but the surprise on her face was nothing to his own. Since when had romantic love featured as even a passing fantasy in his thoughts?

He knew all about dynastic marriages. He'd make one himself one day. He'd tasted love at nineteen and thought his life blighted when his beloved's father had deemed him, the bastard son of a traitor, not a worthy son-in-law. From that day he'd devoted himself to proving himself better and stronger than all his peers.

'No.' Soraya didn't meet his eyes. 'I don't love him.'

Her words hung like a benediction in the air. Zahir's heart felt full.

'But he's a good man. A decent man,' she murmured. 'I owe him my father's life. Without the Emir I would have lost him years ago.'

'So you're repaying the debt.'

She nodded and Zahir had to quell the impatient urge to say the debt had been cancelled with Hussein's actions. It was Hussein who'd owed Soraya's father. But there was no point. He read determination in her fine features. Besides, how could he urge her to go against her conscience?

He could offer her no alternative. Not when he was bound by every tie of loyalty, duty and love to deliver her to Hussein. Not when the alternative would make her a social pariah, an outcast even to her family.

'What of your own dreams? Your aspirations?' The words spilled from him. He'd heard enough about her work to know she needed more from life. The idea of her as no more than a prop to grace Hussein's regal table and be by his side at official functions seemed a travesty. Soraya had so much more to offer.

'My dreams have changed.' Again that small, wistful smile.

'When I was young I had grandiose dreams of helping the nation. Now I…'

She shook her head. 'Now I have the qualifications to do something really useful for our people. I'm hoping the Emir will let me use those skills to support some innovation. We have the resources, and know how in Bakhara to bring power to the outlying regions, for a start.'

'Is that all you want? The good of others?'

Something flared in her eyes, an emotion almost too painful to watch.

'In Paris I'd begun to dream of a different future,' she murmured. 'Where *I* got to choose for myself. I'd follow my career, spread my wings, make my own mistakes.' Her lips twisted. 'I learned how much fun it was to make friends with other women, not because they were from the right families or because we studied together, but because we clicked. I discovered a weakness for philosophical debate and pop music and fantastic shoes.' She lifted her shoulders. 'Nothing earth-shattering or important. Nothing worth pining over.'

Except it was important to her: the right to choose her own path. She'd said as much in his arms on Bastille Day—that there was nothing as important as freedom. He ached at the thought of what she would give up.

'What about you, Zahir? What do you dream of?'

His dreams? Why did they seem less vivid than before?

'Hussein is making me governor of our largest province. It's the province my father misruled as a despot and it will be my job to make it flourish and prosper.'

He waited for the pleasure he usually experienced as he thought of the challenge ahead. The satisfaction of knowing he'd be redressing the depredations of his father.

Nothing came. Not even pride at the fact Hussein valued and trusted him with this important role.

Instead his eyes locked on Soraya's and something swelled between them. An understanding, an emotion he didn't dare name. His body was aflame and the need to touch her again was a compulsion.

Abruptly Zahir stepped back. He kept moving, needing distance before he forgot sense.

He ignored the over-bright shimmer in her eyes and the down-turned curve of her lips as she watched him go. 'I need to talk to our host,' he said.

'Zahir?' He stopped, heart hammering at the sound of his name on her lips.

'Yes?'

'I'm doing the right thing. Aren't I?'

His head whipped round and again that thwack to the solar plexus hit him when her eyes met his.

He breathed deep and searched for the right answer.

He could find none that would satisfy both conscience and desire.

'You're doing the honourable thing.' His voice rang hollow in the silence.

As he forced himself to walk away, he knew for the first time in his life that honour wasn't enough.

CHAPTER ELEVEN

SORAYA paced the luxury hotel-suite, ignoring the view of a quaint Roman square as the sky morphed from peach and bronze to shades of violet and indigo.

Once she'd have watched enthralled, thrilled by the vibrant, fascinating city of Rome. She'd have revelled in today's sight-seeing, the historic sites, the curious byways and above all the people, so full of life and energy.

Yet the city had passed in a blur, overshadowed by the fact this was the end.

The end of her freedom.

The end of her time with Zahir.

Her heart shuddered to a halt then picked up again unsteadily.

Rome was their last stop. Tomorrow they'd board a royal jet that would take them to Bakhara.

Desperation was a coiling queasiness in her stomach, a rusty taste on her tongue, as if she'd drawn blood when she bit her lip.

Tomorrow she'd face the man who would become her husband. She was no nearer finding the equanimity she needed for that than when Zahir had broken the news.

Zahir.

She clutched at a velvet curtain for support, reliving the delicious feel of his hair in her hands as they kissed.

That kiss had blasted away the convenient platitudes she'd

hidden behind. It had revealed in shocking, glorious detail how much she wanted him. How much she needed him.

Heat consumed her. Was she so like her mother? So weak in the face of sexual desire? In the face of love?

Yet this didn't feel like weakness. It felt like strength, light and honesty. A heady euphoria edged with terrible fear that it could never be.

She'd tried to convince herself she couldn't be in love with anyone so aloof and bossy. But the frightening man she'd met in Paris wasn't the real Zahir.

Zahir was proud and inclined to take the lead, but he wasn't a bully. He went out of his way to visit places she had her heart set on, patiently waiting as she combed markets, hunting gifts for her dad and Lisle. He took pleasure in the same things she did, chatting to farmers about the harvest, playing with the local kids. He was warm-hearted and caring. A man generous with his time.

He'd continued her lessons daily till she could swim unaided, determined she'd be safe in the water. He'd stuck to his promise despite the strain of those lessons.

Zahir was excellent company, even if he kept a conspicuous distance from her.

How she craved his touch. His affection.

He felt something for her, she knew it. It was there in his carefully blanked expression and in the fierce, possessive light in his eyes when she caught him off guard.

The memory of that look melted her bones.

She loved him. Yet they couldn't be together. The thought scooped a gaping hole inside her chest.

She was destined for the man who'd given her back her father when she'd been about to lose him. Who'd given her years she'd feared she'd never have. Who'd honoured her with his proposal. By all accounts he'd been a faithful and caring husband to his first wife. Soraya knew he'd respect and care for her. *But it wasn't enough.*

She'd been an innocent ever to think devotion to her country or even her career was enough.

Why couldn't she have love too?

The dangerous thought eddied in her brain.

There were a multitude of reasons she couldn't have Zahir's love. She couldn't ask him to run away with her and betray the man he looked on as his father.

Yet she yearned for him with every cell in her body.

Was it too much to ask for a taste of that forbidden dream? For a morsel to comfort her in the long days ahead when she lived not for herself but for her country and the man who, however decent, could never be Zahir?

Soraya's breath escaped in a whoosh. She'd feared she shared her mother's weakness. But her mother had been in love with the idea of falling in love. Instinctively Soraya knew there'd be no other man after Zahir. He was the one. As for the future— that was immutable. She'd be faithful to the man she married.

But couldn't she allow herself a taste of love to sustain her through a future that loomed barren and bare? Just one night?

Zahir was unbuttoning his sleeves as he pushed open the door to his room. He needed a cold shower. Better yet, a couple of hours in the hotel's gym, then a cold shower. Though he knew it wouldn't help. His mind would be full of...

'Soraya!'

He slammed to a stop just inside the room.

Like an answer to forbidden cravings there she was, standing silhouetted by the glow of a bedside lamp. The soft light lingered lovingly on her ripe figure and his throat closed as all his blood drained south. Her hair was down in dark, rich waves that begged for his touch.

'What are you wearing?' His voice was a hoarse rasp.

She fiddled with the tie at her waist but said nothing. She didn't need to. It was obvious that beneath the embroidered silk wrap she was naked. No strap line marred its smooth texture and she'd done it up so firmly the fabric pulled tight across breasts and hips, cinching in at her waist.

His body raced into sexual overdrive, pulse humming, heat escalating, arousal burgeoning. His breath was choppy as he fought to drag in air.

'Soraya!' Somehow he was walking towards her, though he told himself to keep his distance.

Their gazes collided and he almost groaned at the familiar blast of connection between them.

Her nipples pebbled and his palms ached to reach out and cup the proud bounty of her breasts. Yet he managed to stop a pace away. Desire scorched him. More than desire; a yearning that was as much of the mind as the body. It engulfed him with a force that left him shaking.

'You shouldn't be in here.' It emerged as a plea.

'I couldn't stay away.' She swallowed convulsively and the pulse at the base of her neck raced out of control.

His blood beat just as fast. Just as haphazardly.

How many nights had he dreamed of her coming to him? How many mornings had he lashed himself with guilt over the imaginings he hadn't been able to conquer?

It was wrong. But he couldn't overcome it. He felt too much for her. He wanted her as he'd never wanted in his life. That alone told him how dangerous this was.

Soraya trembled as his gaze devoured her. A muscle worked in Zahir's jaw and she felt the tension come off him in great waves. His hands twitched and she wanted them on her. Surely his touch would relieve the ache deep inside?

'I want to make love with you, Zahir.' A weight lifted off her chest with the words and she dragged in her first free breath since she'd come to his room. 'Please.'

He stood stock-still. If she didn't know better, she'd swear he didn't even breathe.

Fear warred with hope. Grabbing the last of her courage she stepped forward, till the heat of his body encompassed her. Still he said nothing, didn't move a muscle. It was as if he'd locked down, rejecting her and what was between them.

Soraya refused to give in so easily. With a daring she didn't know she had, she reached out and grabbed his hand, placing it on her breast.

Instantly his fingers tightened, cupping her, and she swayed against him, captive to sweet, unfamiliar sensations. Fiery threads unravelled from her breast to her belly and lower, to the place where the ache was strongest and she felt hollow with need.

Gently he squeezed and she moaned as pleasure coursed through her. Much as she'd craved his touch, she just hadn't *known*…

She rose on tiptoe and pressed a kiss to his mouth. But at the last moment he moved and her lips landed on the sandpapery skin of his unshaved jaw.

An instant later his hands bit into her upper arms and he put her from him. Cruel fear invaded her bones as she looked into flinty eyes.

'Don't, Soraya.' His voice was harsh.

'Please, Zahir. I love you.' The words came out in a rush, but she couldn't regret them, even as she saw his head rear back in shock. She put her hands on his restraining arms and felt the muscles bunch and tighten. 'I thought—'

'You *didn't* think!' He almost spat the words as he let her go and strode away across the room. 'How could you even consider coming to my room like this?' He braced himself against the far wall, his head hanging down between wide shoulders that rose and fell with each huge breath.

Despair welled. He was rejecting her.

Soraya knew this was her only chance. She had to make him understand.

A moment later she stood beside him, her hands busy with the tie of her robe.

'What are you doing?' His voice was hoarse.

'Showing you I know exactly what I'm doing.' She paused

and hefted in a shuddery breath. 'It's true, Zahir. I love you.' The whispered words sounded loud in the stillness. 'I didn't want to. I didn't plan it. But I...' Welling emotion choked her. 'I can't pretend it hasn't happened. I can't face the future without knowing just once what it's like to be yours.'

Finally her clumsy fingers managed to unknot the belt. She tore it open and shrugged the silk wrap off her shoulders. It slid down sensitised flesh that tingled as if from a lover's caress.

She jutted her chin high; trying not to cower at the realisation she was naked before his gaze. She felt vulnerable and weak, yet at the same time strangely buoyed, freed for now of the oppressive weight of duty and fear of the future.

Zahir's eyes turned hot and hungry and flames licked her deep inside.

'Please.' Her voice was thick. 'I'm only asking for tonight. Just one night.'

He said nothing. Had she made a terrible mistake?

But Zahir's expression told her she hadn't been mistaken. He did care, did want, just as she did.

She lifted one trembling hand and placed it on his chest. Beneath her palm he felt strong and warm. His heart thudded as quickly as hers. They both felt this yearning. She dragged in a deep, relieved breath and with it Zahir's intoxicating scent.

'Don't!' In a blur of movement he grabbed her hand and threw it off.

Shocked, Soraya stared up at a face of fury. The glitter in his green eyes was lethal, the twist of his mouth scornful.

She backed away a pace.

He followed, his face a mask of contempt.

'Don't think you can come to my room like some...some *whore* and tempt me into betraying Hussein.' His coruscating glare lashed her from top to toe and Soraya shrivelled as if under a whip.

'I thought better of you, Soraya.'

Despite the roar of blood in her ears, she thought she heard anguish in his voice. She must have imagined it.

'You go to your husband tomorrow and it won't be with my touch still warm on your body.' He looked away as if the sight of her sickened him. 'Get dressed and go to your room.' He was still speaking as he strode away and yanked the door open.

A moment later the door of the suite slammed behind him.

Blessed silence descended but in Soraya's head his words ran over and over.

A whore. He'd called her a whore!

With a muffled cry of pain Soraya lifted a shaky hand to her mouth, trying to keep back the bile that surged in her throat. Her legs gave way and she found herself huddled on the carpet.

Hours later Zahir stalked across the square towards their hotel. Even the Italians, who seemed to come alive in the evening, had vanished from the streets.

He was alone. Except he bore in his heart the image of Soraya, naked and impossibly tempting, offering herself to him as if he deserved such bounty.

Soraya, flinching under the despicable words he'd thrown at her in a last-ditch effort to shore up his rapidly failing control, when all he'd wanted was to gather her to him and learn the secrets of her beautiful body.

He felt sick with a pain no distance or mindless exercise could numb. How could he have treated her so? In his heart he'd recognised her desperation and need, for didn't he feel them too? To lash out at her had been more than cruel—it had been unforgivable.

Nevertheless, he'd apologise as soon as she woke in the morning. Before they boarded the plane for Bakhara and her bridegroom.

In the hotel doorway he faltered, his hand going out to steady himself as turbulent emotions threatened to unman him. Grief, loss, shame and unrepentant longing.

'Signor?' The concierge moved forward but Zahir waved him away and made for the lifts.

He'd walked the streets for hours and was no nearer finding peace.

It was past time he returned, even if guarding Soraya from harm on this last night seemed like a contradiction in terms. With her pleading eyes, sweetly feminine body and throaty voice telling him she loved him, she was the most dangerous being on the planet.

She made him believe what he felt was meant to be.

Instead his logical brain reminded himself that he'd eschewed love since he was nineteen, preferring to deal with lust. That she was promised to Hussein. That he owed Hussein everything and couldn't betray him.

His heart was heavy as he opened the door of the suite. The lights were on. Hadn't she gone to bed yet?

He'd assumed she'd be locked in her room. Adrenalin surged at the prospect of seeing her again.

For he wanted—more than wanted. He needed her with every breath of his being. How he'd cope after he delivered her to Hussein, he had no idea.

The door to his room was open, the lights on. Surely she wasn't…? No. It was empty. A shuddering breath escaped. Was it relief or regret that made his heart pump faster?

He turned back into the foyer, intending to turn off the lights in the rest of the suite, when he noticed Soraya's door wide-open.

Frowning, he paced closer. The overhead light blazed on an empty room. A familiar splash of champagne silk sprawled across the corner of the bed, trailing onto the floor. He picked it up, inhaling the scent of wildflowers. The fabric was cold to the touch.

The hair on Zahir's nape rose as he knocked on her bathroom door. When there was no response he jerked it open, only to find it empty.

Apprehension skittered down his spine as his senses went on alert. There was no sound in the suite as he strode from room to room, flinging open doors, hauling curtains back from the wall, even checking cupboards.

By the time he'd rung reception to discover Soraya had left no message, and double-checked every hiding place, he was in a cold sweat.

Returning to her bedroom, he rifled through her belongings: suitcase, clothes, purse and laptop. Even her passport and mobile phone were there.

Where was she?

Zahir scowled at the meagre collection of belongings, as if they could tell him what he needed to know.

Twenty minutes later the hotel had been searched from top to bottom, but there was no sign of Soraya.

Dread curled within him, sending tendrils of fear through his frozen limbs.

He'd done this! With his defensive temper and his unforgivable words. He'd never known such guilt, such fear, as sliced through him now, leaving him bereft and trembling.

Soraya was alone in an unfamiliar city at a time when honest people were off the streets. Only the foolhardy or dangerous prowled the city at this time.

Panic swamped him.

He strode to the window and stared at the empty square as if sheer desperation could conjure her. Somewhere out there, distressed and defenceless, was the woman he'd sworn to protect. The woman he cared for.

If anything happened to her…

Soraya put one foot in front of the other and plodded on. She was near the hotel but the fact she couldn't remember its exact location didn't bother her. She'd prefer never to return.

Yet the future had to be faced.

A hollow laugh escaped her. Weeks ago she'd thought life couldn't get worse than an arranged marriage. She'd fretted over it till she had felt sick with anxiety.

Now she knew what real despair was.

To marry one man while loving another.

To have the man she loved despise her for wanting him.

Pain lanced her and she stumbled, putting out her hand to lean against a stone wall. Even now she couldn't stop trembling.

She couldn't remember dressing or leaving the hotel. All she recalled were Zahir's words.

Had she been so wrong? Did he feel nothing for her?

She bent her head till the world stopped spinning. Maybe the grappa had muddled her senses.

She'd been watching water spurt from an old fountain when a motherly looking woman asked if she was all right. According to her, Soraya had been standing there for over an hour.

She'd led Soraya into a tiny courtyard filled with the scent of geraniums and the rumbling purr of a ginger cat. The woman had invited her to sit then pressed a glass of grappa into her unresisting hands. Then she'd taken the other seat and tilted a lamp towards her embroidery.

How long she'd sat there, Soraya didn't know. She'd lost track of time, soothed by the rhythm of the cat's breathing as it stretched across her lap and the chatter of a late-night radio talk show.

Finally she'd noticed the weariness on the other woman's face and, thanking her for her kindness, made her way onto the deserted street. Now she just had to find her way back. A shudder racked her at the idea of facing Zahir's piercing disapproval. But she had no choice.

After all, what more could he do? Her heart had already splintered into raw, jagged pieces.

From somewhere she dredged the strength to walk on. She'd covered just a metre when a figure came in view. A tall man with a purposeful stride.

Instantly she shrank back, her heart battering her ribs. In her dazed state he looked too much like...

'Soraya!'

He sprinted, his feet pounding the pavement, and before she

could gather her wits to retreat he was there, his hands on her shoulders, gripping her tight.

'Are you all right?' He didn't wait for her answer but ran his hands lightly across her shoulders, arms and face, as if needing to feel for himself that she was whole.

'Don't touch me!' She stumbled back a step till she collided with a wall but he followed, hemming her in.

'Tell me you're unhurt.' His voice was as raw as hers. In the dim light she almost didn't recognise him. He seemed to have aged a decade in one evening. 'Please, Soraya!' His fingers shook as he smoothed the hair back from her face. Something sharp twisted inside.

'I'm fine,' she said over a lump of congealing emotion. 'Don't worry; you don't have to soil your hands by touching me.' Though for one precious moment she let herself believe his concern was for her personally, not because he'd committed to bring her back in one piece.

'Soraya. Don't.'

Before her stunned gaze, Zahir dropped to his knees. He gripped her fingers in an unbreakable hold and pressed fervent kisses to the back of one hand then the other.

'Zahir?' Her befuddled brain couldn't grasp the change in him. To have him literally at her feet was unthinkable. His arrogant rejection was too fresh in her mind. Yet there he was, wretchedness written on his once-proud features.

He made her heart turn over despite her anger.

'I'm sorry.' He looked up, his gaze fiercely direct and a wave of emotion rocked her back on her heels. 'What I said to you.' He shook his head. 'It was unforgivable, as well as being untrue.'

His hands tightened and with a sense of wonder she read desperation in his grim visage.

'I lashed out because I felt myself crumbling.' He tore in a ragged breath that pumped his chest hard. 'Every word you spoke pulled me closer to deserting my principles, my duty, my loyalty. You *scared* me.'

He shook his head, though his eyes never wavered from hers. 'I wanted you so badly—*still* want you—it was torture having you offer yourself when I was so weak.'

'You want me?' Her heartbeat stalled.

'How could I not?' His voice was hoarse, his breath hot against her hands. 'I've desired you from the moment I saw you in that club. Every day and every night you fill my waking thoughts as well as my dreams. Soraya. Can you ever forgive me? To call you that...' His breath shuddered out in a rattling rasp. 'You were being honest, when I couldn't even face what I felt.'

He threaded his fingers through hers, turned her hands to plant heated kisses on her palms. Tremors of sensation shot up her arms, to her breasts and down to her womb. Her knees shook so hard she thought they'd give way.

'What do you feel, Zahir?' Soraya was light-headed, overloaded on emotion. She gripped his fingers hard, knowing it was only the current of energy flowing between them that gave her strength to stand.

'This.'

He was on his feet, looking down at her with an expression that melted her bones. His palms were strong and warm on her cheeks, his breath a ripple of heady pleasure as it caressed her lips.

Instinctively her lips parted as, with a groan, he lowered his mouth.

Their lips met and the world exploded. Caution vanished, incinerated by the fierce need devouring them.

Soraya sagged against Zahir, clinging to his broad shoulders as he took her mouth in a kiss that devastated and fulfilled. It pulsed with raw, unvarnished desire and sweetest longing. Soraya couldn't get enough.

His body pressed against hers from thigh to chest, imprinting her with his heat, his hunger. And she was just as eager. Just as unrestrained.

Their lips mashed as she kissed him with more fervour than

expertise. He gathered her close, his hands proprietorial as they stroked down her back till she arched high against him, eager for greater contact.

An instant later he stepped back, despite her moan of protest. Before she could complain, he hoisted her into his embrace and held her close to his pounding heart.

'Not here,' he growled in an unrecognisable voice that set off sparks of excitement deep in her belly.

He turned and strode towards the hotel, a man on a mission. 'We need privacy.'

CHAPTER TWELVE

ZAHIR'S hold remained unbreakable as they entered the suite and the door crashed closed behind them.

Soraya carried jumbled impressions of the hotel foyer and the gawping receptionist's stunned expression, though Zahir hadn't slowed his purposeful stride long enough for her to feel anything but excitement at his possessive hold.

The mirrored lift to the penthouse suite reflected Zahir's granite-set visage, his jaw angled in a way that warned he'd brook no interference. No wonder the receptionist had stayed safely behind his desk.

Zahir's expression sent a wave of pleasure coursing through her. A purely feminine pleasure of anticipation.

His pace didn't falter as they crossed the suite's foyer. Lamp-light beckoned them into his room where light spilled across the sprawling bed.

Zahir slammed to a stop and in the quiet Soraya heard only their breathing, merging like a single heartbeat, fast and eager.

'Soraya.' It wasn't Zahir's voice; not the easy, calm voice she'd come to know. This sound was dredged from the depths of a tortured soul.

She shivered luxuriously as it wrapped around her, connecting to a deep, visceral part of her.

This was unknown territory yet the world had never felt so right as in his arms. Doubt and uncertainty fled before the force of them together: Zahir the epitome of conquering male, and she all melting, wanting female.

He lowered her to her feet, sliding centimetre by slow centimetre down his taut frame till she was strung so tight with need she could barely stand. She leaned in, latching needy fingers around his strong neck so she could feel his hot flesh.

That simple contact was almost unbearably wonderful.

'If you don't want this, say so,' he groaned, his lips a caress against her hair that set a whole new set of nerve endings into spasms of delight. 'Soraya!' His chest expanded mightily as he dragged in air. 'I can let you go but you have to tell me. Now!'

The way his big hands claimed her hips, pulling her up against him so she felt the rigid length of his erection, it seemed impossible he'd ever release her. Yet she knew his formidable will-power.

'No! Don't let me go.' Part demand, part plea, her words were harsh in the thundering silence.

Don't let me go, ever.

For ever. That was how long she wanted Zahir. She needed him in her life always.

She loved him with a raw, soul-deep passion that cut so deep she knew she'd carry it with her the rest of her life.

Soraya felt a great sigh of relief pass through him and recognised the unsteadiness in his touch—it was the same for her. Zahir needed her so vehemently, so completely he burned up with it. His flesh was hot beneath her fingers and tremors coursed his body.

A lifetime's reserve and caution disintegrated under the onslaught of feelings that welled free at last. Zahir's hot skin against her fingers was a benediction. She watched his brilliant eyes, heavy-lidded and mysterious as he drank in the sight of her.

The way he looked at her...

She slid her hands to his collar and with one quick tug wrenched it open.

His chest, contoured muscle and flesh dusted with dark

hair, beckoned. Her heart galloped as she spread her fingers wide, learning him.

My love.

She leaned in, breathing deep the intoxicating essence of him. Of the man she loved with all her being.

'Soraya.' She felt the breath rise in his chest as his voice trailed across her skin. Still their gazes locked.

The world stopped as they trembled on the brink.

Then, with magnificent disregard for her wardrobe, Zahir copied her action. Yet when he took her dress in his big hands and yanked, the silk ripped. It tore so far it was the work of a moment for him to slide it off her shoulders. The fabric slithered down her body in a furtive caress that made goose bumps prickle her flesh.

She hardly noticed, for the look in Zahir's eyes blotted all else from her mind.

Words poured from his lips, a whispered stream of praise and thanks as his gaze followed her dress down, then rose again to her now-rosy cheeks. That hoarse litany of heartfelt appreciation was enough to make any woman blush.

'No woman is perfect, Zahir.'

Why she demurred, she didn't know, except perhaps that he overwhelmed her. She wished she could be perfect—for him. The heated intensity of his stare, the guttural depth of emotion in his voice made her feel for a moment like the goddess he described.

How could any woman live up to that?

'Yet you are perfect, *habibti.*' He looked into her eyes and she felt that half-familiar shudder rip through her from the impact of an unseen force. 'To me you are.'

The glow in his eyes made her heart swell.

He said more but it was muffled against her throat as he kissed her. She tilted her head back in ecstasy and he lashed an arm around her waist to keep her from falling.

Yet she fell. Into a vortex of tumbling emotion and sensations.

It wasn't just the pleasure of his kiss. It was the way he made her feel: treasured, appreciated, loved.

This time when his hand cupped her breast it wasn't at her clumsy invitation. Zahir's was an expert's touch, moulding, caressing, teasing till wildfire roared through her to rush in a whirlpool of heat between her legs.

Her hands slid to the smooth flesh of his shoulders as he bowed her back, further and further, till she lay draped across his arm. His mouth closed over her breast through the filmy lace of her bra and she whimpered in delight, her fingers clutching at him frantically.

'Zahir.' Did that low, keening throb of sound come from her?

'You have no idea how much I want you.' His lips moved across her breast and throat as he spoke. 'I've tried to resist but I'm only human.'

'I don't want you to resist,' she gasped.

'Just as well.' He licked her nipple and her breath clogged in her throat. 'I couldn't stop now to save myself.'

She felt the mattress beneath her and when his arms came away from behind her they dragged her bra too. Dazed, she watched it arc over Zahir's shoulder as he stripped her panties and shoes away.

She should feel nervous as he ate her up with his eyes. Despite a lifetime's modesty, she couldn't. Not when the pride and pleasure in his expression made her feel like a queen.

He braced his arms wide and a shiver of delicious trepidation shot through her at the sensation of being surrounded by such a virile, dominant male. But, instead of lowering himself to her, he retreated down the bed.

Anticipation hummed through her, knowing that soon, when he'd stripped his trousers off, they'd...

'Zahir?'

'It's all right, little one.' His deep voice reassured but she couldn't relax, not when he settled himself deep between the V of her legs, splayed wide by his gently insistent hands.

'What are you...?' A hiss of indrawn breath clotted the

words in her throat. First his hand and then his mouth stroked her there, where need throbbed strongest.

Soraya's whole body jerked hard, as if from an electric shock. But this was pleasure, pure pleasure so intense it overwhelmed her senses.

One caress, another, and she almost lifted off the bed, held in place only by Zahir's solid weight as a shower of sparks ignited in her blood.

She needed to escape, keep some fragment of control, but delight as well as his imprisoning body kept her there, splayed and open before him.

Her eyelids drooped. Her mouth sagged as she gasped in another raw breath and suddenly, like a roiling tide that grew till it blotted out the world, ecstasy engulfed her. She shook and sobbed with the force of it, abandoned to a delight so intense she could never have imagined it.

A delight of Zahir's giving. Through the maelstrom her hand gripped his where it rested on her thigh. That was her lifeline, her connection to him.

Finally, as she lay spent and gasping, he slid from her grasp. She roused herself to protest, but the press of his mouth to the flesh above her hipbone stifled her words. Just the touch of his lips there evoked a pleasure she should be too spent to feel. His hands skimmed her lightly and she shifted under his touch, like a cat curving into a petting hand.

Except Zahir's hands moved with deliberate, erotic delicacy that soon had fire running in her veins again.

'Come to me?'

At her husky plea, his head lifted. Soraya's heart somersaulted as she saw how the skin dragged taut over those strong features. His eyes held a febrile glitter that spoke of fierce yearning.

'Not yet.'

'Why not?' She grasped his shoulders and tried to haul him close. It was like trying to loosen bedrock. 'Please.'

'I can't.' He shook his head. 'I have no control left. Once I…'

'Don't you understand?' Her voice shook. 'I don't care about subtleties or control. *I need you.* Just you.'

Soraya's heart gave a great leap as she read relief in his face and eagerness. She watched, mesmerized, as he reared up, dragging his clothes off.

She'd seen his body before at the pool, but now, in the golden glow of the lamp, he was hers. Her gaze lingered on the strong, lithe form of the man she loved. Even his scars, reminders of the dangerous life he'd led, seemed precious. Her pulse raced as she read the taut power in his heavy thighs, the wide span of his shoulders and the arrogant jut of his erection. As she stared he smoothed on protection.

She licked her lips, her mouth dry. But as he prowled up the bed, caging her with his body, Soraya felt no hesitancy, just gratitude and fizzing anticipation.

A mew of delight escaped her as he settled over her. To feel his chest against hers, the fuzz of his hair tickling her nipples, the smooth heat of his belly against hers—she hadn't known that alone would be bliss.

Hands tunnelling through his thick hair, she kissed him with all the love and wonder burgeoning within. His response was all she could have hoped for. Tender yet urgent, lavishly satisfying, even as her body stirred anew at the masculine weight pressed high between her legs.

'Soraya.' It was a groan of need as he centred himself above her.

'Yes.' She kissed him feverishly, holding him tight, almost afraid to believe this was real.

Then anticipation shattered, as with one surging movement he thrust sure and strong.

Her eyes sprang open. She was stunned by his overwhelming weight, the fullness that surely was impossible despite being so patently real. She was pinioned in a way that made something like panic rise and spread.

Her breath hitched and she forgot how to breathe as her body locked in shock.

She heard Zahir's heartbeat, loud as her own, fast as her own, and his laboured breathing, harsh in the stillness.

Dazed, Soraya groped for the pleasure that till a second ago had hummed in her needy body. She found only blankness.

'Breathe, *habibti*.' Zahir nuzzled the tender skin below her ear. 'Breathe for me.'

It wasn't his command that broke her stasis but the tiny shimmy of delight raying from the point where he kissed her.

He kissed her again, taking his time to lave her pulse-point and she dragged in a shuddering breath, her chest rising beneath his. Her skin tingled at the friction between their bodies and her next breath was deeper, filled with the male scent of him.

Zahir insinuated his hand between them to touch her breast, plucking delicately at her nipple, and a judder of heat rippled through her. Her frozen limbs eased a fraction and her stunned rigidity eased, replaced by a different, delicious tension.

Slowly, lavishly, Zahir seduced her mouth with his till the hint of panic eased.

'That's my girl. It's all right, see?' He moved, withdrawing from her little by little, till she missed the press of his body above hers and even the strange, too-full sensation of his possession.

Instinctively she slanted her pelvis and he responded with another thrust, this time claiming her body centimetre by slow centimetre. Now the sensations he wrought brought fire to her blood and a different sort of tension.

'Zahir!'

He lifted his head to see her face. To her shock he looked to be in pain, his features pinched. Yet his eyes blazed with a brilliance that stole her breath all over again.

Her hand lifted to his cheek. Tenderness filled her as she read what it cost him not to take as his body dictated, but to harness his impulses.

'Tell me what to do.' She felt so useless.

His lips quirked in a brief smile that looked more like a grimace. 'Lift your legs.' He nodded as she complied. 'Higher. Around my waist.'

Soraya tentatively followed his instructions as Zahir once more slid away, then back with an ease that evoked a stab of pleasure.

Her eyes widened. 'That feels...'

'It does, doesn't it?' His eyelids drooped till she saw only slits of dark green. One more easy thrust and this time she anticipated him, rocking up and back with Zahir, eliciting another sharp pulse of pleasure.

She tightened her hold, wanting to comfort him even as another rush of erotic sensation undermined thought.

They rocked together, finding a rhythm so excruciatingly slow it alternately stoked her arousal to fever pitch and satisfied it with a blinding flash of searing pleasure. The pleasure was the greater for seeing its reflection in Zahir's face.

Each dazzling, joyous pinnacle was shared so intimately it seemed they were one, their bodies moving in tandem, their minds linked as they shared something profound.

Finally, after what seemed a lifetime, pleasure crescendoed. Soraya's eyes fluttered shut and she clung to Zahir as, with a rush, their mutual climax splintered thought in a crash of crystal shards.

The sound of her name on Zahir's lips echoed through the velvet darkness that claimed her.

Zahir paced back from the bathroom into the darkened bedroom.

Was she asleep? He hoped so. He had to think, had to come to grips with what they'd done.

What *he'd* done.

Never, since the day Hussein had rescued him from his father, had Zahir acted on pure instinct without thought or plan.

Never had he acted solely on what he felt.

Until now.

Even at nineteen, when he'd fallen hard for the daughter of

the palace's head groom, he hadn't behaved rashly. He'd thought himself in the throes of love yet he'd never put a foot out of line, courting carefully, respectfully—till her father had put an end to his aspirations, rejecting him as too young, too lacking in prospects, the son of a dishonourable man.

Yet as Zahir neared the bed and saw Soraya, her hair a lush curtain that allowed glimpses of her silvered skin in the moonlight, he felt more than ever in his life.

He wanted her, craved her with all the longing in his battered heart. A heart she'd reawakened.

He wanted to drown out the world in the heady pleasure of her soft embrace.

He wanted that searing sense of rightness, of homecoming, of ecstasy as he became more than just the man he was, stronger for being part of Soraya.

Something tugged hard in his chest as he halted by the bed. He groped for control. Then her eyes opened, dark and fathomless as a desert sky. Her lips curved in a smile so tender it made his heart throb in a new, unfamiliar rhythm.

'Zahir.' The whisper of her sweet voice saying his name was devastating as an earthquake. He trembled at the impact. When she reached out to him that last, almost-sane part of his brain shut down.

He snatched her hand, cupping it so he could press urgent kisses to her palm. Her luxuriant ripple of pleasure was enough to dislodge any foggy shreds of sanity.

'Soraya.' His voice was raw with all he felt and could no longer deny.

Then he was with her, flesh to flesh, his rough body grazing her softness, his aching groin against her tender belly. He tried to hold back, to restrain himself, but she confounded him, her lips at his throat, stalling his breath in his lungs. Then her hand, small and smooth, curled around his erection and his heart stopped.

He surged against her palm, unable to prevent himself, revelling in her gentle, clumsy hold that was more erotic than that of the most practised seductress.

Zahir tugged her close, hands sliding on rippling tresses and satiny skin.

Now she found her rhythm, encircling him in long strokes that drew him tight and rigid as a bow.

It was ecstasy so potent it bordered on agony.

'You have to stop.' He reached for her hand. The rest of his words dried as he held her, holding him. A great shudder passed through him as he groped for something, anything, that would stop him succumbing.

'You don't like it?' Doubt or excitement in her voice? He couldn't tell over the drumming pulse in his ears.

She moved and the caress of her long hair over his shoulders and down his heaving chest drove his desperation to new levels. Her skin, her voice, her hair, her touch; everything about Soraya destroyed him. His limbs lost their strength, his resistance shattered, as she pressed her lips to his collarbone and chest, her nipples grazing his belly in swaying strokes that drove spikes of raw need through him, puncturing resistance and good intentions.

His hands fisted in her hair, holding her tight as she slithered lower.

Her tongue flicked him gently, tasting him, and he bucked, helpless beneath her. Only his grip on her scalp remained strong.

Her lips opened and he was lost.

CHAPTER THIRTEEN

IT WAS late when Soraya woke. She knew without looking that Zahir had gone. She sensed it, just as she always knew when he was near.

Through the night and the early hours they'd lain in each other's arms, always touching. The sound of his breathing had lulled her to sleep after their tumultuous lovemaking.

Her skin glowed, her heart sang, her body throbbed with a pleasurable ache. Her limbs were heavy as if they'd never move again, yet at the same time light, as though she still floated on a plane where nothing existed save herself and the man she loved.

She opened her eyes and saw it was broad daylight. Her heart missed a beat.

She'd tasted bliss but now the real world intruded. She'd known for one short night what it was to be in the arms of the man she loved.

How could she give that up?

She had no choice. Nothing had changed. All the reasons they couldn't be together still held sway. Zahir knew it too. He'd already gone.

Desperate to see him, she flung off the sheet and rose. Her knees wobbled, weak after last night's loving.

A surge of heat tingled from her feet up to her face. Last night there'd been no embarrassment or thought of modesty, yet this morning, without Zahir's embrace, she found she could still blush.

Her clothes were tumbled on the floor. Instead of wearing them, she hurried to the wardrobe and grabbed the robe hanging there. She fumbled as she shrugged it on and cinched it tight. Her fingers as well as her legs shook.

She needed to see Zahir, to cling to the magic just a little longer, before she closed the door on love for ever.

Just one look, one touch.

He was in the living room, fully dressed as he stared at the busy square below. Disappointment stirred as she took in his wide shoulders in the dark jacket, his powerful legs hidden from view in tailored trousers.

He looked so…formal. After last night's potent virility, these clothes made him appear curiously stiff.

She was halfway across the room when he swung round, an espresso cup in his hand. Her pace slowed as he lifted the cup and took a long sip.

He looked different. It wasn't just the clothes. There was an aura around him that reminded her of the fiercely self-contained man he'd been in Paris.

She blinked as shyness assailed her. How could she be daunted by his business clothes? This was Zahir. The man she adored. The man who, she knew in her heart, loved her too. Given his strength of character nothing but that could have prompted him to spend the night loving her as if there was no tomorrow. The knowledge was poignant pleasure and pain intermingled.

'Good morning.' Her voice was husky. The last time she'd used it was when she'd cried out his name in the throes of passion.

'Good morning.' His black eyebrows were a horizontal smudge above severe features and he gave no answering smile. 'How are you feeling today? Are you all right?' His quick concern warmed her. Zahir had been a demanding lover, passionate, but incredibly tender.

'I feel fabulous.' She refused to think of how she'd feel when it was time to say goodbye.

Soraya's steps faltered and her heart lurched as her eyes locked with his. She found blankness there where before there'd been passion, love and even—she could have sworn—wonder. Ice water trickled down her spine.

'What's wrong?' He held himself so rigidly.

His mouth twisted in a brief, brutal smile that spoke of pain not pleasure. 'You can ask that?'

'Has something happened?' she whispered. 'Is there news from Bakhara?'

His fingers clenched so tight on the coffee cup she thought its handle would snap. 'No news from Bakhara.'

Soraya hefted in a sigh of relief, her hand pressed to her chest. For a moment, reading his serious face, she'd wondered if something had happened to her father.

'You look pale, Soraya. You must be worn-out. Why don't you go back to bed and rest?' He took a couple of paces towards her then pulled up short as if yanked back by an invisible rope. The sight of him stopping that telling distance away made every hair on her body rise. His gaze shifted towards the bedroom and colour streaked his sharp cheekbones. 'You must be sore. Last night I should have…'

'Zahir, I'm okay, *really*. I'm just…' What? Feeling needy? She knew their time was almost over and needed Zahir's embrace just one more time to give her strength to do what she must.

She moved towards him then slammed to a stop as he retreated.

It was just a half-step and he covered it quickly, pretending to cast about for somewhere to put his coffee cup, though there was a table right beside him. Yet she couldn't mistake his instinctive movement.

Her heart crashed against her ribs as disbelief swamped her. She grabbed for the back of the sofa to support herself.

'We need to talk,' he said before she could speak.

She nodded. She could barely believe this was the man she

knew. He was so ill at ease and distant. As if last night had never happened.

Or as if he regretted what they'd done.

A knife twisted in her vitals.

Had he been disgusted by her enthusiasm or her untutored clumsiness? She squashed the idea as absurd. Last night had been indescribable pleasure for both of them. The love between them had made each touch, each sigh, magic. It had been so much more than simple physical gratification.

Soraya flushed at the memories, but another look at Zahir's sombre face made the blood drain from her own.

She told herself he only did what he had to—created the distance that must forever more be between them.

Yet her poor heart yearned for one last touch, one embrace, one whispered word of reassurance. How weak she was.

'I'll make the necessary arrangements. You can leave it all to me.'

'Arrangements?' She tilted her head.

'For our wedding.' His gaze meshed with hers, but Soraya saw only flinty determination in eyes that looked curiously flat. 'In the circumstances it will be a small ceremony, and soon.'

'Wedding?' The word emerged as a breathless gasp. She couldn't be hearing this. Yet a flutter of excitement rippled through her, sabotaging her determination to be stoic as she faced the future.

'We're getting married.' She knew that determined look. He was a man set on a course of action and nothing would deter him. The flutter became a tidal wave of excitement.

'But we can't. There's no way...' She spread her arms, encompassing all the reasons they couldn't be together.

'After last night we must.' Strangely he didn't smile at the memory of what they'd shared. 'I've spent the morning working out a way we can be together.'

'It's impossible.'

'I'll make it possible.' A thrill ripped through her. Zahir would move heaven and earth to achieve what he wanted. Was it possible, after all, that there was a way for them to be together? She hardly dared believe it.

'I'll speak to your father as soon as possible and do my utmost to persuade him this will be in your best interests.' Zahir drew in a breath that made his whole chest rise, as if readying himself for some Herculean task.

Her dad. 'I'll talk to him.'

If there was explaining to be done, she'd do it. He'd be horribly disappointed, and worried—not to mention embarrassed that the royal engagement was off—but he loved her. Surely, eventually, she could make him understand, especially if Zahir had a plan that would lessen the fallout? After all, he understood love.

'No.' Zahir shook his head and straightened his shoulders to stand ramrod-straight. Soraya was reminded of a soldier on parade. 'It's my duty. I'll deal with it.'

It. He made news of their feelings sound like a crime. Soraya clasped clammy hands together as the nervous gyrations of her stomach grew worse.

She understood how dreadful this would be. The shock and dismay they'd cause with their relationship. The gossip. The scandal. But despite it all the promise of a future with Zahir at the end of the trauma made exultation bubble through her veins. For it seemed Zahir believed there really could be a future for them. Despite her best intentions excitement swelled.

No matter what sacrifice it took, she was ready. Nothing was more important than the love they felt.

Yet, she realised now, Zahir looked not like a uniformed officer so much as a man facing a firing squad.

'It's not about duty, Zahir. My father will understand better if I explain.' She wanted to take his hand but he'd shoved his fists deep in his trouser pockets.

What was wrong? If he'd found a way for them to be honest about their love…

His grim expression doused her excitement.

He did love her, didn't he?

The way he'd murmured endearments last night, the fact that he'd taken her to bed despite all she knew of his honour-bound code of conduct, had convinced her he shared the same deep emotion she did.

'Zahir?'

'Of course it's about duty.' Zahir's jaw clenched so hard his face looked painfully tight. A laugh jerked from his lips. The sound of it made the hairs on her nape prickle. 'I was going to say it's a matter of honour, but I have no claim to honour now. Not after last night.'

Raw pain stared out from his face as he turned to her and the bright, fierce joy she nursed close to her heart dimmed. Sensation plunged from her chest right down to her abdomen, like a lift plummeting to catastrophe.

'Of course you do.' She hauled in a difficult breath. 'Last night was about honesty and—'

'Don't!' The harsh syllable stopped her as she leaned forward. 'I dishonoured you last night. And I dishonoured Hussein.' Zahir tugged one hand free of his pocket and rubbed it round the back of his neck as if in pain. 'Not to mention your family and myself.'

Soraya's arm slumped to her side. She told herself it was natural he felt guilty. He wasn't the only one. Even now she felt torn.

'You didn't dishonour me. I chose—'

'Not dishonour you?' His bark of laughter was ugly. 'You were a virgin, Soraya. That privilege should have been your husband's.'

Frantically Soraya fought for calm, reminding herself he only spoke as many in Bakhara did.

'It wasn't a privilege, Zahir. It was a gift. *My* gift.'

He swung away as if he couldn't bear to look at her. 'Do you think I'd have taken you as I did if I'd known?'

Soraya froze. Her labouring lungs atrophied as his words sank in.

She opened her mouth and closed it, grasping for words.

Finally she dredged some from deep in her pain. 'You thought I'd already lost my virginity so it was safe to sleep with me?' A great tearing gasp ripped through her, widening with every second he remained silent. 'You're only offering marriage to make good the damage you've done my reputation?'

'No. Of course not.' Yet his face when he swung around wasn't that of a lover. It belonged to a stranger. A stranger who looked at her and felt only horror for the consequences of what they'd done.

He'd wanted her last night, but not enough to withstand the cold, clear light of a new day. There was no joy on his face at the idea of their future together.

No thought of *them*. Just of duty and dishonour.

Dishonour. The word tainted what they'd shared so gloriously.

What she'd thought they'd shared.

Soraya had shared everything. Herself, her hopes, fears and dreams. Her love.

And Zahir? He regretted last night with a fervour that couldn't be faked. Could it be that he'd shared no more than his virile body? She'd blurted her love for him but he hadn't, even in the most intimate of moments, reciprocated.

Finally she realised how significant that was.

She watched him turn to pace the room, his expression brooding. She had to know the truth. Yet still she hesitated, scared of what his answer might be.

'Zahir? Do you...*care* about me?'

His head jerked up. 'Care?' His brow pleated as if she spoke a foreign tongue. 'Of course I care. I want to *marry* you, Soraya. I want to look after you and protect you. Be assured, I will make it all right.'

All right. Hardly the words of a man in love. He made no mention of joy or anticipation.

Wave after wave of shock passed through Soraya. Her knees weakened and she plopped down onto a nearby chair. The leather was cold against her trembling palms.

Would she ever feel warm again?

That's what love gets you. Nothing but trouble!

Soraya shook her head, as if she could banish the voice of doubt in her head.

But she knew it for the truth. Soraya had always feared love with good reason. Wasn't that why an arranged marriage to the Emir had originally seemed such a safe, appealing option?

She looked up at the man with the closed face, pacing with such ferocious concentration. She couldn't focus on his words over the swelling roar of blood in her ears, but she could make out his tone: cool and clipped. No passion. No emotion. None of the love she'd been so sure he felt.

He was in damage-limitation mode. As if she was a diplomatic tangle to be sorted out. An indiscretion to be dealt with.

Her heart gave a single frantic thud that shook her to the core. To have him hold out hope to her of happiness and then dash it was the cruellest torture of all.

She'd do anything, go anywhere with him, if only he'd ask. *If only he loved her.* But she refused to be nothing more than a mistake to be rectified.

She'd thought his actions were proof of deeper feelings. Yet he'd never spoken the words. Never claimed to love her.

Marrying a man who felt compelled to 'do the right thing' by her could only lead to disaster. Zahir would end up resenting her and she—could she cope with loving him and knowing he didn't feel the same?

'Soraya?' She wasn't listening to him. Zahir jolted to a stop, his gaze straying over her: so sweet, so vulnerable in that oversized robe.

His woman.

Despite the untenable situation he'd put them in, he couldn't help but glory in the fact she was his. Incontrovertibly. Totally. His.

Wildfire shimmered in his blood as he remembered how they'd been together. He wanted to thrust the world aside and lose himself in her. But he had to be strong for both of them. He couldn't contemplate a future without her.

That meant dragging himself far enough away, mentally and physically, to be able to confront the implications of their passion. Touching her would addle his brain. It was imperative he think clearly. Besides, he had no right to touch her until he'd made this right for her.

He had to deal carefully with her family, the public and, above all, Hussein if Soraya was to be able to hold her head up in public.

His lungs squeezed tight as he thought of Hussein. Scalding guilt drenched him.

No matter what he felt for Soraya, nothing excused what he'd done. To Soraya. To his friend and mentor.

She might brush it off as 'honesty' but he knew it for selfish weakness. A strong man would have held back, waited till they got to Bakhara, then declared himself publicly.

What sort of man was he?

He'd prided himself on his loyalty, courage and honour. He was weak to the marrow, a hollow sham of the man he'd believed himself. His loyalty to Hussein, his honour, his intentions, had all disintegrated before Soraya.

Had he fooled himself when he'd pretended he wasn't his father's son? That he was stronger, better, honest? Surely his betrayal of Hussein was far worse than his father's disloyalty? *He was his father's son after all.*

The knowledge threatened everything he knew of himself, his life and aspirations. Yet he couldn't afford to dwell on that now. Not when Soraya needed him.

It hadn't been enough to dress, to avoid touching her, to force himself to focus on the ugly public repercussions. All his efforts to strengthen himself ready to face what must be faced crumbled before her potent presence. He wanted to shun the world and take her back to bed. But the world wouldn't go away.

'Soraya?'

Finally she looked up. Yet it was as if she didn't see him. Her gaze was unfocused, fixed on something far away.

She opened her mouth and spoke, but his brain refused to process what she said. He gazed blankly down at her, willing her to break the nightmare horror that suddenly engulfed him.

He crouched before her, hands planted on the leather sofa on either side of her, trapping her close.

'What did you say?' His voice was a hoarse crack of sound.

Her gaze shifted as if she couldn't bear to meet his eyes. His heart pounded. 'I said I won't marry you.'

Zahir stared, vaguely aware that he was still breathing despite the gaping hollow where his heart had been. How could that be?

'No!' Finally he found his voice. 'You must!' She was his. What they shared had transformed him. Made him realise there was more to life than honour, challenge and duty. What in his youth he'd imagined to be love was nothing compared with this all-consuming emotion.

'Must?' She arched a brow imperiously, like the princess Hussein wanted to make her. Her voice was cool, distancing him. 'You have no right to talk to me about *must*. You may be my bodyguard but you're not my keeper.'

Zahir reeled back on his heels, shock slamming into him. Fire exploded in his belly and crackled along his arteries at her attempt to fob him off.

Fury such as he'd never known blasted through him. She couldn't deny him!

'I'm a hell of a lot more than that.' Fear roughened his voice. He leaned in again, close enough to inhale her scent and feel the rapid flutter of her breath on his face. 'You smell of sex, Soraya. Did you know that? Of my skin on yours. My seed.'

Her eyes rounded, her reddened lips parting, and Zahir wanted more than anything to kiss her into capitulation. Seduce away the idea that they couldn't be together.

Instead he reached for the collar of her robe.

'Here.' He yanked it aside to reveal her collarbone. 'I've left my mark on you.'

He'd felt guilty when he'd realised his unshaven jaw had marked the delicate skin of her throat and breasts.

Now all he felt was primitive satisfaction. Despite his anger and shock, his erection surged against the confines of his clothes. He wanted her with every searing breath in his constricted lungs. Not just the sex. He wanted *her*: the woman who'd changed his life and taught him how to feel.

She shoved his shoulders so abruptly he almost lost his balance. As it was she had time to surge to her feet and stride away across the room before he scrambled to stand. He made to follow her and then stopped, reading the pain on her face. An ache filled his chest.

'So we had sex.' Her voice was bitter, unlike anything he'd ever heard from her lips. 'What do you want? Your name tattooed on my skin?'

He'd settle for her smile. Her heart beating next to his. The knowledge she'd be with him, always.

He shook his head. This wasn't Soraya. Not the loving, generous woman he knew. What had gone wrong? He'd worked so hard, spent hours working out how they could be together permanently, and she was throwing it all away.

'You said yourself last night wouldn't have happened if you'd known I was a virgin.' Contempt dripped from her words.

'No!' He paced closer. 'I said I wouldn't have taken you like that. So clumsily.' He waved a slashing hand at the thought of his uncontrolled possession. 'I should have been gentler.' He'd seen the shock of discomfort on her features, read it in every tensed centimetre of her body, and still he hadn't been able to pull away.

The closed expression on her face proclaimed she didn't believe him and he couldn't bear it. He strode across the room, reaching for her.

'No. Don't touch me.' She shrank back.

Instantly he stopped, his belly churning sickeningly.

'Soraya, please. I don't know what's wrong, but we need to talk. To sort this out.'

'Talking won't help.' Her long hair rippled around her shoulders and breasts, reminding him of the sensual delight they'd shared. 'There's nothing to sort out.'

'How can you say that?' Had the world flipped over on its axis? Everything was scrambled. Everything he felt, everything he thought she felt, turned on its head.

'Because there's no future for us, Zahir.'

For long seconds she gazed into his eyes and he read regret there. Regret and pain that tore him apart because he was helpless to stop it. Or did he imagine it? Now her expression was blank and austere.

'Of course there is. If you'll just listen. I've worked out a way—'

'There's no future because I'm going to marry the Emir as planned.'

Zahir swayed on his feet as his world imploded, collapsing around him.

'No! No, it's not possible.' He struggled to draw breath, to banish the wave of blackness that threatened to engulf him. 'You're not serious?'

But her face was set in determined lines. This was *real*. One of the things he loved about Soraya was her honesty. She meant it.

'You *can't* marry Hussein. Not now.' Not when they'd found each other.

'Why not?' Her chin tilted and her dark eyes, once soft as pansies, flashed fire. 'Because you plan to tell him I'm no virgin?'

Zahir shook his head.

'You said you loved me.' The words were torn from him. A desperate appeal in the face of pure torment.

She said nothing. His aching heart longed to hear the words again, to feel the balm of her love surrounding him once more.

Still she remained silent.

Had they been mere words? Lies?

She'd never lied before, screamed his battered soul.

'I'm going through with my betrothal,' she said at last.

He wanted to yank her into his arms and make love to her till she sobbed his name and clung to him, till she recanted and said she wanted him, not Hussein.

But the seed of knowledge he'd nurtured so long had finally burgeoned into full blossom. Once before he'd sought marriage and been rejected because he was the son of a miscreant, with no prospects. He'd vowed then to work harder, be stronger, more successful than any of his peers. To make a name for himself that would be respected.

He'd thought he'd succeeded. And it was true that his reputation, his talents, his position, had been won by sheer hard work and devotion to duty.

A duty he'd failed abysmally last night. Just as he'd failed the tests of loyalty and integrity.

Soraya had said she wanted to make the most of her last days of freedom. Now she'd tasted forbidden fruit. She'd sated her curiosity and her desire for him.

She'd made her choice. Zahir was good enough for a fling, a night's pleasure before a lifetime of fidelity.

But to marry the illegitimate son of a notorious traitor when she could have Bakhara's ruler? Why settle for less than the best?

Why settle for a man who'd proven himself without honour?

Zahir turned on his heel and strode from the room.

CHAPTER FOURTEEN

INSTEAD of escorting Soraya to the palace, Zahir found himself superfluous as her father, ecstatic at her return, met them at the airport and took her to their home.

A courteous man, he invited Zahir to accompany them for refreshment, but Zahir refused.

As for Soraya, she thanked him with formal courtesy. Raw pain skewered him as he watched her treat him like a stranger.

As if last night hadn't happened.

As if they meant nothing to each other.

But she wasn't an accomplished actress. Zahir didn't know whether to be buoyed or furious when he saw, for an instant, the betraying wobble of her lower lip. Her stiff, angular walk, unlike the gentle sway of her natural gait, told him she wasn't as indifferent as she pretended.

Then why…?

'Sir?'

Zahir turned, recognising one of the palace servants.

'Sir, the Emir asks that you attend the council chambers as soon as possible. The negotiations over disputed territories have commenced and you're needed.'

Zahir turned towards the main concourse. Through the glass doors he saw a royal limousine waiting. Yet he had to force himself not to follow Soraya and her father instead.

'Sir. It really is urgent.'

Zahir frowned. 'I'm sure the Emir is well able—'

'That's just it, sir. The Emir is away in his desert palace. He'd expected you earlier and in the meantime left the negotiations to his diplomatic staff.'

Zahir's frown became a scowl. Hussein was in the desert? Odd behaviour from a man expecting his bride-to-be. After a decade-long betrothal, surely he was eager now to claim the bride he'd ordered home?

'The Emir…' Zahir lowered his voice. 'He is well?'

His companion nodded. 'Yes, sir. So I understand. If you'll just come this way…'

It took two full days to turn the talks around into something productive, another day to develop an agreement for consideration by the various nations and a day to ensure the delegates were farewelled with formal courtesy.

Despite the heavy load placed on his shoulders, Zahir performed his official duties as if by rote. He was distracted. Tormented.

By Soraya, who'd said she loved him, only to reject him. Who'd turned from searing passion to icy detachment.

By the puzzle of Hussein's behaviour when he remained uncontactable during these vital discussions. It wasn't the action of the forthright, capable man he knew.

But, above all, by his own turbulent feelings.

Four days neck-deep in sensitive, world-changing negotiations and he'd felt none of his usual pleasure in a difficult job well done.

His priorities had changed.

Because he'd fallen for a woman who meant more to him than the life he'd carefully constructed. What did any of it matter when Soraya was denied him? Worse, when she herself denied what they'd shared?

Pride shredded, desperation welling, he could find no equanimity, could barely maintain a pretence of it.

Now, on the fourth night since his return, he finally had the luxury of solitude. Instinctively, he'd turned to the desert.

Behind him stretched the glittering city, lighting up the night. Before him, the moon-silvered open ground of the wilderness. He urged his horse forward, inhaling the evocative scent of wild herbs, dusty ground and the subtle indefinable scent of exotic spice borne from the east.

As they picked their way into the desert a perfume teased his senses, of some night-blooming flower, rare and fragile.

It reminded him of Soraya and her delicately perfumed skin, sweet as mountain blooms. Of her beauty and grace, how she made a simple smile a thing of rare joy. His heart crashed against his ribs at the thought of never seeing it again. Or seeing her smile at another man: Hussein.

Pain tore at him like great talons ripping his flesh.

It wasn't just her beauty or her smiles he wanted. It was her love. The way she made him feel. When she'd said she loved him, something inside had glowed incandescent: a hope, a dream he'd never known existed until Soraya.

She'd seduced him not with sex but with the wonder of herself. A woman like no other. Proud, determined, prickly, emotional, giving, warm-hearted, loyal. Loyal to the father she loved and the man to whom she'd promised herself.

But not to him.

Hadn't she felt the same joy at his love for her? Hadn't she—?

The horse whinnied and skittered to a halt as Zahir yanked on the reins.

She *must* know how he felt. It had been there in his every desperate caress, in every breath, each murmured endearment. His desire for marriage.

Yet, reeling back time to that night, the morning after, it struck him that he'd never said it aloud. Never declared his feelings.

He shook his head. Of course she knew he cared for her. Why else would he strategise so frantically to find a way they could wed?

But did she know he loved her?

He sat unmoving so long the stars wheeled in the darkness overhead and the moon inched towards the horizon. Finally his patient mount shifted and Zahir let him have his head, cantering down a slope into the network of valleys that marked the border of the great desert.

When finally they stopped, Zahir had reached a decision.

It was beyond him to believe he could win her for himself, though he couldn't completely stifle a sliver of outrageous hope. Yet he had to act. He had to declare what he felt so Soraya knew and Hussein too.

It wasn't in Zahir's nature to hide behind silence.

Suddenly Soraya's words about honour and honesty made sense. What he felt, however problematic, was honest and real.

He'd been honest with Hussein all his life. It was his honesty above all that had built his reputation as a man who could be trusted, especially in matters of state. He couldn't change now. He couldn't face his friend and benefactor hiding what he truly felt.

He couldn't let Soraya turn from him without knowing.

He couldn't live a lie. Not even if it meant banishment and loss of both the prestige he'd built and the dreams he'd held. Loving Hussein's wife doomed him to leaving all he'd once held close, even his best friend.

He would lose everything.

Yet hadn't he already lost the one thing that mattered?

He turned the stallion and headed back to the city, his heart lighter than it had been since Rome.

The royal audience-chamber was vast, richly ornamented and exquisitely decorated with murals and mosaics of semiprecious stones. Designed to reinforce the majesty of the nation's ruler, it could hold hundreds.

Zahir stopped on the threshold, surprised to find it virtually empty with only a few score in attendance.

There was Hussein, looking stately as ever and reassuringly fit, greeting guests. To one side was Soraya, gorgeous in amber silk with a gilt embroidered veil covering the back of her head. She was pale but composed.

His heart jerked with mingled delight and pain.

Would this be the last time he saw her?

After this he'd no doubt be escorted to the border and never allowed to enter the country again, much less approach the royal presence. The trembling in his belly spread to his limbs and for a moment he doubted he had the strength to go on.

Moving his gaze, he saw Soraya's father, hovering close to her. The rest of the guests he recognized: the country's most influential leaders, tribal elders and government ministers. Men he dealt with every day. Men he respected.

Men who'd shun him when this was over.

He watched Hussein, the benevolent, extraordinary man who was as precious to him as a father. Who trusted him implicitly. His stomach dived as he thought of the yawning rift he'd create between them and the hurt he'd cause.

Shifting his gaze back to Soraya, warmth stole through him. Not the heat of lust. This was stronger, fuller and more profound.

Taking a deep breath, he strode towards his fate.

Soraya held herself stiffly, beset by doubt.

She'd never been in the audience chamber and its brilliance daunted her, reinforcing the Emir's power and wealth. Reminding her she was to marry a stranger, as unfamiliar to her as the opulence that surrounded them.

When summoned to the palace this morning, she'd almost welcomed the invitation. For, despite what she'd told Zahir in her pride and hurt, she was less convinced than ever that she could marry the man who held centre stage in this auspicious gathering.

Yes, he was generous and decent, good-looking too, if you had a penchant for much, much older men.

But he wasn't Zahir.

It didn't matter that Zahir didn't love her. She'd given her heart to him and she knew that, like her father's, her love once given could not be rescinded.

She'd hoped for a chance to talk with the Emir in private. He had a right to know his bride loved another.

Instead she and her father had been ushered into a formal reception of VIPs so daunting she'd had difficulty doing more than respond to polite greetings. She very much feared the purpose of the gathering was to introduce her formally as a royal bride and announce a wedding date. Why else was she included amongst all these eminent people?

As soon as this was over she *had* to find a way to speak with the Emir privately. She owed him the truth, though she cringed, thinking of the consequences.

A stir in the crowd caught her attention. Heads turned towards the grand entrance. At the same time a frisson of awareness scudded down her spine, drawing her flesh taut and tingling, as if she'd been dipped in fizzing champagne.

Her breath caught. That sensation was unmistakeable.

It was Zahir. No one else made her feel that way.

Despair flowered deep inside as she realised there was no escape. She'd hoped to put off this first public meeting till she'd gathered her defences more strongly about her, ready to project an aura of disinterest.

Would she ever be able to pretend so well, when just the knowledge he was in the room made her knees weak?

Unable to resist, she turned and there he was, his long legs eating up the marble vastness as he strode towards the throne.

Her pulse rocketed as she took him in. Zahir as she'd never seen him. Zahir in a pure white robe that flowed from broad, straight shoulders, loose trousers tucked into traditional Bakhari horseman's boots. A belt secured a curved scabbard for the customary knife.

There was nothing ostentatious about him. His clothes were simple but of the finest materials. Yet no other man in the room matched him for sheer presence and masculine magnificence. Not even the Emir.

Zahir's face was drawn in harsh lines, as if he'd just come in from the blinding desert sun. Or as if he had momentous matters of state on his mind.

'Zahir! Welcome.' The Emir moved forward to greet him, arms outstretched for an embrace.

'My lord.' Zahir stopped several paces away, bowing deeply.

The Emir halted, his brow pleating as if Zahir's formality surprised him. 'It gladdens my heart to see you, Zahir. You are well?'

'I am, sire. And you are in good health?'

Soraya listened to the exchange of greetings with half an ear, all the while bracing herself for the moment Zahir looked past the Emir and noticed her. Would he come and greet her, or simply nod, as passing acquaintances might? She didn't know which would hurt more.

She must have missed part of their conversation. For suddenly the Emir was ushering him forward and Zahir was shaking his head.

'Before the business of the day begins, I have something I must tell you.' Zahir's eyes, like polished emeralds, flashed straight to her, pinioning her where she stood. As ever, she felt the impact of his gaze from the roots of her hair to the tips of her feet in their embroidered silk slippers.

So he'd known she was there all along.

She shifted, a sense of terrible premonition welling.

'Of course.' The Emir gestured for him to continue. 'You are among friends. Let us hear what is on your mind.'

Zahir turned back to the Emir, his facial muscles so taut she wondered if he was in pain.

'It concerns the lady Soraya.'

Her heart skated to a halt then took up a quick, faltering rhythm. A murmur of interest resonated around the room but she barely registered it. Her whole being focused on Zahir.

What was he going to do—broadcast what he considered her shame to all and sundry? Accuse her of disloyalty? Unworthiness?

She found she'd clasped her hands together, fingers entwined and shaking. Her feet were rooted to the spot.

'Go on.'

'There is something you should know before you marry.' Zahir paused and you could have heard a pin drop in the massive room.

Soraya's father reached out and touched her arm but she couldn't tear her gaze from Zahir.

What was he doing? Why?

Her stasis shattered and she stumbled forward, her long dress sweeping around her unsteady legs.

The Emir half-turned to acknowledge her as she joined them. Yet Zahir didn't shift his gaze. He stared straight ahead at the man he'd called his best friend and mentor.

As if he blocked her out.

Panic swirled up from her stomach, prickling its way through her whole body. Or was it pain? The ache of waiting to be betrayed by the man who'd stolen her heart?

'I know you prize loyalty,' Zahir continued.

'I do.'

'Then you should know that I can no longer remain in Bakhara. Not once you marry this woman.' Zahir's voice was firm and strong, eliciting a ripple of gasps and whispers from the assembled group.

Heat roared through Soraya's cheeks then receded, leaving her cold and strangely empty. Then she felt the clasp of a sustaining hand on hers as her father moved to stand by her. That proof of his love almost shattered her, knowing how unbearably disappointed he would be at the news Zahir would break.

She opened her mouth but no sound emerged.

'Why is that, Zahir?' On her other side the Emir sounded unperturbed, as if he couldn't read the dark sizzle of emotion in Zahir's eyes or the thundering pulse at his temple.

'Because I love her.'

Silence descended, broken only by the rattle of Soraya's breath in her overburdened lungs. Surely she imagined the

words? For Zahir to say them now, here, in front of the nation's
elite… She tried to take it in but couldn't.

'I love her,' he said, louder this time, making himself heard
over the immediate clamour of protest that rose around them.
'Therefore I can't be part of your court. I can't remain here, a
loyal subject, when she—' he swallowed hard '—is your queen.'

Zahir's gaze flickered to her and she read haunting anguish
in the depths of his eyes.

Her heart gave a great leap, battering up against her throat.
She felt light-headed.

'You have never been precipitate before, Zahir.' The Emir
spoke over the swelling roar behind them. 'I counsel you not
to make rash statements now.

'Soraya?' At the Emir's questioning tone, she dragged her
gaze to the weathered, stern face of the older man. 'What are
your feelings for this man?'

He spoke with a gravity that confirmed all her fears for
Zahir. Had he destroyed in one moment everything he'd worked
for? She knew how much his position, his work—and above all
this man's regard meant to him. Dismay gnawed.

She sensed the horror of the onlookers and knew he'd just
willingly given up all he'd strived for. For *her*.

Yet she couldn't stop the elation singing in her bloodstream.
Her lips curved in a smile she hadn't a hope of hiding.

'I love him.' She turned to Zahir. Pulling free of her father's
hold, she stepped closer to the man who stood poised as if for
battle, alone against the crowd. 'I love him with all my heart.'

She no longer heard the others. No longer noticed the older
men. All she knew was the dawning light in Zahir's clear gaze.
The pride and love that softened his severe features as his eyes
devoured her. The sweet joy that filled her.

She could scarcely believe it. *He loved her.*

Not only that, he had declared it in defiance of protocol, of
tradition, of everything that stood between them.

How long they remained there, gazes enmeshed, cocooned

from the uproar, Soraya didn't know. Finally the Emir's voice penetrated. He spoke in deep, carrying tones.

'My kinsman Zahir's announcement has rather pre-empted my own. I've brought you all here today as witnesses.'

Soraya spun around, alarm rising. He couldn't mean to continue with the wedding now? *Surely* he couldn't? She started forward in protest but a hand stopped her.

'Wait, Soraya.' It was Zahir's voice in her ear, quelling the worst of her panic. His fingers engulfed hers and she squeezed back. If they were to be parted now...

Her face flamed as she faced the crowd, read the strain on her father's features and the avid curiosity of so many strangers.

The Emir spoke again. 'I called you here because it's been my intention for some time to abdicate.'

Shocked silence greeted his words. Zahir's fingers spasmed on hers and she heard his swift intake of breath.

'That decision will affect others.' He turned and Soraya found herself meeting kindly hazel eyes. There was no trace of the anger she'd anticipated in his face.

'In the circumstances, it would be unreasonable of me to ask my betrothed to feel committed to me now I've taken a decision which will so substantially alter her future.'

He was letting her off the hook?

A buzz of questions and protests surfaced but Soraya couldn't take them in. All she could process was the solid warmth of Zahir beside her, his strength flowing into her from their linked hands and the knowledge she was free.

The Emir raised a hand as he turned back to the crowd and silence fell. 'I have of course thought carefully about a successor. A man of my own blood. A man who has proven himself capable and trustworthy in so many capacities. A man who just this week saved our peace negotiations when they were in danger of foundering.'

He turned and all eyes followed the direction of his gaze. 'I propose Zahir Adnan El Hashem as my most worthy successor.'

* * *

Soraya paced the antechamber, oblivious to its luxurious fur-
nishings and breathtaking view over the city. What was hap-
pening? Her nerves crawled with impatience. She'd felt revolt
in the air back there, fuelled by shock and Zahir's uncompromising stance over her.

Her father had ushered her here, away from curious eyes,
while the future of the nation was decided. He'd been stunned
by the scene in the audience chamber. But, once she'd confirmed she really was in love, he'd proved staunchly supportive, only leaving when she forced him to go and take his part
in the deliberations.

The door to the antechamber opened and Soraya swung
round, ready to throw herself into Zahir's arms. His eyes met
hers, glittering with raw emotion, and her heart juddered in
the aftershock of that connection.

He loved her...

But he wasn't alone. The Emir walked beside him.

Soraya clasped her hands together and forced herself to be
still, dread rising as she saw Zahir's grim expression and the
Emir's weary one.

'How could you do it?'

Soraya opened her mouth then realised the question came
from Zahir's lips and that he was standing in front of the Emir,
legs planted aggressively wide.

'It was necessary,' the older man said.

'Necessary!' Zahir's deep voice rose to a pitch she'd never
heard before. He sounded on the verge of violence. 'You *used*
her.'

'I regret that.' The Emir cast her a troubled look.

'Regret?' Zahir's hands fisted at his sides. 'You shackled a
young, unsuspecting girl to you with no thought of what that
might do to her? How *trapped* she might feel? How distressed?'

Soraya rushed forward and grabbed his arm. It trembled
with repressed fury. His other hand covered hers possessively
and she leaned into him, still dazed by the fact she could. He
wanted her, loved her.

The tension in Zahir's strong frame shocked her. As if it would take just one careless word to unleash violence.

His anger on her behalf was like a comforting blanket, reminding her she wasn't alone any more.

'I'd lost my wife, the love of my life,' the older man said, his voice hollow. 'I think now you both have some idea how that felt.' Soraya felt a quiver of distress pass through Zahir. Or was it through her? The thought of losing him now she'd finally found him made her clutch tighter.

The Emir heaved a deep sigh. 'To rule, I had to be married.' His gaze shifted to Soraya. 'Or betrothed.'

He spread his hands wide. 'You remember how things were then, Zahir, how unready the nation was for another ruler. And there was no logical successor.' His lips quirked. 'Though one young man had caught my eye. I knew with experience one day he'd make a fine emir.'

'The illegitimate son of a brutal tyrant?' Zahir's words bit like bullets.

'The honourable, capable man I'm proud to call kin, however distant the connection.' The Emir paused. 'I've been weary a long time, Zahir. A ruler needs a helpmeet. I'm ready to retire to my country estate and study the stars, read my books and watch your children grow.'

Heat suffused Soraya's cheeks at his direct look. The idea of carrying Zahir's babies made a pulse beat deep in her womb.

'But Zahir isn't married. How could you know…?' Her voice trailed off in the face of the older man's smile.

'I knew Zahir would have no trouble finding a bride. It's time he was settled.'

But Zahir wasn't to be distracted. 'You brought Soraya into an untenable situation.'

The Emir nodded. 'I'd planned today to annul the betrothal on the grounds of my abdication. That would leave Soraya's reputation unblemished. I hadn't anticipated your announcement.'

'But it doesn't go anywhere near making up for the trauma she suffered.'

'Zahir!' She tugged at his arm. 'It's all right now, truly.' And it was. Miraculously, it was. She'd have gone through far more than anxiety over her royal betrothal if it meant having the man she loved.

He turned and looked down at her. His breath on her face was a soft caress. The look in his eyes sheer heaven.

'I owe you my deepest apologies, Soraya.' Dimly she was aware of the Emir bowing, but she couldn't tear her gaze from Zahir's. The way he looked at her was like dawn's fresh promise after an endless night. A moment later the door snicked shut and they were alone. Finally.

'Is it true?'

Zahir lifted her hand and kissed it, turned it over and pressed his lips to the centre of her palm. Lightning jagged through her veins and lit up her senses. His eyes glinted with promise, like cool oasis water in the desert.

'It's true, my love. I adore you. And I'll never let you go.' His voice dropped to a gruff bass rumble that made her insides melt. 'If you'll have me.'

'But in Rome…'

He pressed a finger to her lips.

'In Rome I was a fool. I was so caught up making plans and anticipating problems I forgot the most important thing of all: love.' He smiled and a sunburst exploded in her heart. 'I've wanted you since the night I saw you in Paris.'

'But wanting isn't love.'

'And I've loved you almost as long. The more I learned about you the less I could resist.' His finger on her mouth moved in a slow, seductive stroke along her bottom lip that sent delight shivering through her. 'The question is, do you want me?'

Stunned, her eyes widened. 'Of course I do. How can you doubt it?'

'Because right now the royal council of elders is debating whether I should become Emir of Bakhara. It's by no means a done deal, and there'll be a lot of negotiating, but I need to know what you think. You didn't want a royal life. You wanted more than royal duty and who can blame you?' He paused and gathered her close so her heart beat against his, that single pulse all the stronger for being shared. 'I'll step away from it if that's what you want. I couldn't accept without your agreement.'

'Zahir!' She pulled away as far as his encircling arm allowed. 'You can't do that. You're made for the position.' She couldn't imagine anyone better suited. The knowledge filled her with pride. 'Unless you don't want it?'

Green eyes held hers, unblinking. 'I won't lie. The challenge of it is all I could ever want. Except for you.' His voice deepened and sent threads of gossamer silk trawling over her sensitive skin till she quivered. 'I'd rather have you, Soraya. That's my choice.'

Her heart swelled as she stopped his words with her lips. 'Then it's just as well you don't have to choose.' Something inside broke at the thought he'd give up all he'd worked for if it meant keeping her. She felt humbled. At the same time determination filled her. She'd be the best wife an emir could have. 'I'd rather be yours than anything else in the world, my darling.'

'You'll be mine? Even if it means being wife to the Emir?' His voice was raw with disbelief. His hands shook as he pulled her closer. 'You can pursue your engineering, whatever you want. It won't be all duty. I swear.'

She cupped his beautiful, questioning face in her hands, marvelling that he was hers. 'Well, there will be hardships, I know. Think of all the shopping I'll have to do to look the part if you're made Emir. The shoes, the clothes...' Her breath escaped in a gasp as his marauding hands investigated the sheer silk of her bodice. 'Zahir!'

'The attentions of your virile husband?'

'That will never be a hardship.' Soraya smiled with all the joy in her heart. She couldn't believe the world could hold such happiness.

'Just as well.' His head lowered, blotting out the elegant room, and the world faded away.

EPILOGUE

THE oasis encampment vibrated with the hoof beats of so many horses, all beautifully caparisoned, all bearing horsemen in traditional garb. Their white robes shimmered in the moonlight, their heirloom weapons glinting.

The women had just left in a fleet of luxury four-wheel drives back to the capital.

Soraya's breath caught at the spectacle of Bakhara's strongest and finest wheeling their horses out of the oasis.

The slightest of breezes feathered her dress and she shivered, not with cold, but with delight at the scene that wouldn't have looked out of place in some old romantic tale. An instant later warm hands clasped her arms, pulling her back against a strong, solid body.

A sigh of pleasure escaped her lips. It had been so long, a month in fact, since she'd felt Zahir so close.

Even through her silks and his fine cottons, his heat branded her. She snuggled back against him, revelling in the possessive tightening of his grip, the hitch in his breathing and his burgeoning hardness against her buttocks.

She shimmied back as delicious languor filled her.

'Minx,' Zahir growled as a salute of rifle shots thundered in the night sky. 'Wave for our audience, *habibti*.'

Soraya lifted her arm then moaned softly as he ground his pelvis hard against her. Rills of desire ran through her body, pooling deep inside.

The last of the riders disappeared over the ridge, leaving them sole occupants of the oasis.

'I thought today would never end.' Zahir's lips were hot on her neck. 'Why do Bakhari weddings take so long?'

She turned, wrapping her arms around his neck.

'Not any wedding. The Emir's.'

His hooded eyes glinted in the light of the nearby braziers. 'No regrets, my love?'

'None. Except...' She chewed her lip, feeling delight shimmer within as Zahir's hungry gaze honed in on her mouth. It was a wonder she didn't explode from the heat.

'What?' A frown pleated his brow.

'Except you're wasting valuable time talking.'

With a grin that stole her heart all over again, Zahir scooped her into his arms and strode into the richly decorated tent. Antique lamps spilled multicoloured light over thick, silk rugs, embroidered cushions and the widest bed Soraya had ever seen raised on a dais at the centre of the space.

Tenderly Zahir laid her on the satin cover, then propped himself beside her.

The lamplight cast his strong features in bronze, highlighting their severe strength and above all the shimmering emotion in his eyes.

Soraya's heart welled, reading the reflection there of all she felt.

'Your wish is my command, lady. But be warned.' He nuzzled the base of her neck as his fingers slid over the thin silk of her dress. Delicious tension bowed her taut body. 'I intend to tell you often how much I love you.'

It was a promise he kept through their lifetime together.

* * * * *

ROMANCE

MEDICAL

0912 GEN STD HB

Mills & Boon® Large Print

October 2012

ROMANCE

A Secret Disgrace	Penny Jordan
The Dark Side of Desire	Julia James
The Forbidden Ferrara	Sarah Morgan
The Truth Behind his Touch	Cathy Williams
Plain Jane in the Spotlight	Lucy Gordon
Battle for the Soldier's Heart	Cara Colter
The Navy SEAL's Bride	Soraya Lane
My Greek Island Fling	Nina Harrington
Enemies at the Altar	Melanie Milburne
In the Italian's Sights	Helen Brooks
In Defiance of Duty	Caitlin Crews

HISTORICAL

The Duchess Hunt	Elizabeth Beacon
Marriage of Mercy	Carla Kelly
Unbuttoning Miss Hardwick	Deb Marlowe
Chained to the Barbarian	Carol Townend
My Fair Concubine	Jeannie Lin

MEDICAL

Georgie's Big Greek Wedding?	Emily Forbes
The Nurse's Not-So-Secret Scandal	Wendy S. Marcus
Dr Right All Along	Joanna Neil
Summer With A French Surgeon	Margaret Barker
Sydney Harbour Hospital: Tom's Redemption	Fiona Lowe
Doctor on Her Doorstep	Annie Claydon

0912 GEN STD LP

Mills & Boon® Hardback

November 2012

ROMANCE

A Night of No Return	Sarah Morgan
A Tempestuous Temptation	Cathy Williams
Back in the Headlines	Sharon Kendrick
A Taste of the Untamed	Susan Stephens
Exquisite Revenge	Abby Green
Beneath the Veil of Paradise	Kate Hewitt
Surrendering All But Her Heart	Melanie Milburne
Innocent of His Claim	Janette Kenny
The Price of Fame	Anne Oliver
One Night, So Pregnant!	Heidi Rice
The Count's Christmas Baby	Rebecca Winters
His Larkville Cinderella	Melissa McClone
The Nanny Who Saved Christmas	Michelle Douglas
Snowed in at the Ranch	Cara Colter
Hitched!	Jessica Hart
Once A Rebel...	Nikki Logan
A Doctor, A Fling & A Wedding Ring	Fiona McArthur
Her Christmas Eve Diamond	Scarlet Wilson

MEDICAL

Maybe This Christmas...?	Alison Roberts
Dr Chandler's Sleeping Beauty	Melanie Milburne
Newborn Baby For Christmas	Fiona Lowe
The War Hero's Locked-Away Heart	Louisa George

Mills & Boon® Large Print

November 2012

ROMANCE

The Secrets She Carried	Lynne Graham
To Love, Honour and Betray	Jennie Lucas
Heart of a Desert Warrior	Lucy Monroe
Unnoticed and Untouched	Lynn Raye Harris
Argentinian in the Outback	Margaret Way
The Sheikh's Jewel	Melissa James
The Rebel Rancher	Donna Alward
Always the Best Man	Fiona Harper
A Royal World Apart	Maisey Yates
Distracted by her Virtue	Maggie Cox
The Count's Prize	Christina Hollis

HISTORICAL

An Escapade and an Engagement	Annie Burrows
The Laird's Forbidden Lady	Ann Lethbridge
His Makeshift Wife	Anne Ashley
The Captain and the Wallflower	Lyn Stone
Tempted by the Highland Warrior	Michelle Willingham

MEDICAL

Sydney Harbour Hospital: Lexi's Secret	Melanie Milburne
West Wing to Maternity Wing!	Scarlet Wilson
Diamond Ring for the Ice Queen	Lucy Clark
No.1 Dad in Texas	Dianne Drake
The Dangers of Dating Your Boss	Sue MacKay
The Doctor, His Daughter and Me	Leonie Knight